Elementary

Luminaries

by

Darla @ Makenlief

DEDICATION

I dedicate most of this illumined work to both my mother, Della Arms, and my late husband, John G. Also, to people who encouraged me by trying to understand and by challenging me.

My mother was an amazing artist and thinker, sensing more in small spaces than most people ever ventured trying to imagine.

John Goldsworthy, my late husband, is absent but widely felt, and his enduring spirit continues to guide all who loved and knew him closely.

During this book's most recent edit, I offered my gratitude with regard to Mike while imagining appreciation to Dave and Anthony. A belated thank you to Mary Jo, Paula and Charles.

I applaud those who unceasingly are open to fresh, innovative ideas. Humans who dream, create, and write always will value honesty and openness, and that's a trusted place where I can hone and strengthen my own creativity and intuitiveness.

Elementary Luminaries is for formerly reluctant adult readers, young-at-heart adults, maturing adults, and all who've recently awakened to the bountiful opportunities there are witnessing a myriad of simple complexities within every situation.

Elementary Luminaries

Questions of Adventurous 'Detourists'
by
darla @ makenlief

Illustrated by
darla @ makenlief

978-1-7338458-2-3

ACKNOWLEDGEMENTS

Though incorporating fragments of already widespread ideas and/or philosophies, with sprinkling traces of spiritual beliefs, the weaving worked, with the author not upholding or promulgating one system over another, not endorsing rigidity of religious dogma.

This novella was conceived around the 2020 pandemic and went through its renovations. Although fiction though the author felt it was a true story, as any creator could, especially how the 2020 pandemic affected. All characters' names are fictional.

There is no explanation of the portmanteau "detourist," in the story. Makenlief pays tribute to those who might struggle and ponder on personal paths while managing to maintain their distinct light so brightly - not for others to simply see **them,** but to illuminate to inspire others to be their own distinctive 'light.'

Mid November 2020

Barely noting Rudy's bronze colored jeep scooting ahead of her new identical gifted one, his car phone buzzed out a very loud song. A roughly homemade ring that sang an unheard of lyric 'Fawny,' as his jeep's top folded down.

Rudy adjusted his inscribed *'Fawn Me'* visor.

Preparing something?

A scene to top off last night's episode? Rhetta's self-confidence at appetizer time flattened, mixing the overrated taste of slimy oysters with a thick gut-wrenching state. She was confused. Noting the customers' stunned reactions to his embroidered, *Fawn Yourself.'* shirt, she wondered if he was ever a hired showman. Nothing resembled what she had envisioned of him.

The Santa Barbara gates met with a whisper as twin jeeps eased out to intimidate clusters of sidewalk joggers -- some startled by the brash phone rings then took in Rudy's punning visor - this had no stored social more to draw on, so they stoically trudged on but wondered about the intention. Dog walkers hid amused ridicule, toggling glances at cell phones.

Now Rudolf Marcher's console speakers blared louder. A young man's voice blurted his name. This driveway was likely a frequent venue, she thought, he was too at ease on this stage.

So, a lot in the last 24 hours had floored her and now uncomfortable as heck inside a cushy jeep she'd never want, the glove box receipt revealed fully purchased with her name as the owner. So quickly. But starting how and when and because of what, exactly? She was dizzy but needed clarity.

Prompted months before when employed at the community center and because she'd read contents in her late sister's diary, that's it. Her desires to be important? Widely notable? Yet avoid being a weirdo or communal narcie if it happened for her?

1

Kelli, her much older half-sister, died a year before, bequeathing Rhetta a modest fund. A box and a cashier's check. Decades of Kelli's yearly diaries, bound in pristine floral painted leather. 'RM' was Kelli's unrequited torch. Rudolf Marcher.

Yes, Rudy, the mega… so far is quite rich - in spacy oddity.

What had happened between the two back then? She had to know. A weekend dive into diaries materialized after one struggling week of grant writing for the community center.

Cursive blue ink on ageing diary paper wasn't explicit. Kelli's contented marriage and widowhood were at times overshadowed by something else. Several allusions were strong. Rudy's and her high school puppy love was brusquely pruned by her parents.

That was Rhetta's only info beyond the ink written "RM" in little poetic verses here and there, repeatedly in the diary.

The half-sisters never lived under the same roof. Rhetta, 25 years younger, was born during their dad's second marriage. One holiday when both dined with Dad, Kelli reminisced aloud about that teenage crush, Rudy, who starred in a high school musical and had danced and twirled a cane- all off-sync. He sang, 'I adore you,' focusing on the empty seat beside Kelli's – not connecting to her eyes. The talk then was how strange he'd even gotten the role.

Now today Rhetta decided she'd give him another chance to listen to her pitch. At breakfast. She couldn't go home until seeing this through. She'd spent months being challenged, learning causes, and today still held graciousness her sister's long-ago tie brought this appointment. He was a builder, a planner.

And now her teeth were grinding.

In her rearview mirror, the greenest, plushest lawns of the Marcher's huge complex overbore its cool and brief luxury she'd never need, and never really want. Just like this jeep.

He hadn't missed a beat studying Rhetta, though, and fully understood the reason for her visit. She'd proven herself as

2

forthright. Had acutely concealed perplexment. His jeep gift brought mystery of his intent, wanting to see her next move.

'To honor the memory of Kelli' was his stated reason.. Then when stating "no romance with me," she felt herself buckling. Ha ha. That would be difficult! With him being married, her being unattracted, and his inability to connect to her eyes. His pupils pointed at her nose, toggled shortened glimpses aiming at her jawline, or ear lobes. All through dinner.

Dating was not her motivation; she'd responded. Was this really happening? Ludicrous? *'Return the jeep, your bold naivete brought this convolution,'* practicality butted in. The meal nose-dived. They drove both jeeps back to the mansion, with her hating in having to learn how, and they didn't speak again until this morning.

Now, in bright morning sunlight, he was eager and out and leaning on his jeep bumper peering at his growing sidewalk audience. The phone caller's young and cocky voice was too loud for anyone to miss a syllable, "Hey there, Rudy! it's Tyler here, heyyy! How y'all doing? I am contacting all you one-percenters."

"Calling the wha, what, *ONE* percentile?"

Marcher interrupted. "No gain for you, Bud. You won't get even one percentile of my attention. No further comment from me about the correctness of half a percentile. Top, baby! R*ight now, delete* my cell number… He smiled when giving this command.

Rhetta felt again the prickles inhabiting her spine.

Nothing so far resembled her hoped-for outcome. She'd learned he hadn't competed during high school either academically or in sports. No one ever imagined he'd achieve any successes. Though young, cute and compliant, he would too often blurt hard-to-swallow axioms, hitting nerves and testing blatant social stigmas.

Rudolf's parents weren't educated, his dad sold bricks, his mom was a seamstress, affording nothing above a community college for him. Both died before Rudy met his wife, Dena, who instrumentally helped him see industry timing was on his side after acquiring his PhD. Together they'd earned enormous success.

One recent diary entry revealed how Rudolf's wife, Dena, was fading with illness. That diary entry matched the span of time Kelli was processing her own advanced cancer diagnosis.

The year before, in 2019, Rhetta learned through her center's colleague that a woman named Mrs. Dena Marcher donated millions toward health, education and shelter causes – but it went to adjacent county center. Funds were intended to assist lower middle incomed citizens who weren't qualified for poverty level benefits.

Rhetta's center's programs needed that level of help. She decided today she'd put the jeep up for sale so to donate funds. They'd be grateful and happy to hear from her again, too. She resigned it all months ago to work on this presentable research.

Nationwide, many low-income people were embittered. They weren't poor *enough* for Medicaid -- or anything like food stamps or cash. Lower-middle class citizens achingly realized this unfairness. Mrs. Marcher's donations focus on shared housing for lower middle-class seniors, as well as childcare and education.

Now almost nine o'clock and Rhetta continued studying how he moved, now leaning, supported by the bumper housing his right knee, arms crossed but holding the cell. He faced his audience now wearing a jacket bearing: *'I'm so Fawning Hilarious! Rich in ideas, Rich in Spirit, Rich beyond the other 99.1 %.'*

Why try stopping his practice of contradictory oddities? This attracted converse, that's why. He also didn't fret over how much a misfit he'd been. He saw Rhetta trying to figure him out.

"I'm not a mere one percenter!" Rudolf blasted.

So inappropriate, so unnecessary. She sank thinking this all meant she'd wasted months researching for approval from a wacko.

Too late to find a normal rich person? Can he even level with her?

"Rudy, can you please exchange the jeep for an advertisement on a billboard that reads: *'Needing a billionaire colleague to manifest what research has found to do. Lower middle class must have fair treatment.'*"

Her cell gave a link for urban lingo. 'Fawning', and it meant '*to stroke, to act admirably toward, gush over*'...adoration of oneself, be adored. An emerging level of a 'narcissism' tagged world?

Striving to become a powerful focus wasn't a new dance.

Marcher knew what she was likely going through, his honed zig-zagged, tailored offbeat approach was to shake kilter. He saw how she managed it. She was different; he'd been learning for months.

LUMINSTRATUM

A faint purplish fog blanketed by twinkling stars backdropped David Anthony and My Lady, who sensed each other without audibles or sight while sharing - the way of their celestial corps.

David Anthony: That is you, My Lady? Dear one!

My Lady: David? Anthony? Hello! I'm to record.

David Anthony: Yes, again they've got us on planet earth. Good to be attending again with you, My Lady. As spirit.

My Lady: Not cloaked with matter now. Other celestials' tales about occurrences while surveilling lives are brilliant! Now, we're here!

David Anthony: Our label here is sentinel? Why can't it just stay unlabeled helpful spirit?

This world called earth by the English speaking has other celestials noting there's high anxiety here regarding exchange/money.

My Lady: We overlapped while humans! I am not 'your lady' as you call me now. I was 'Dear Lady' to you, remember? We share span layers. Our training never ends. I know you by your essence, and we'll soon see more definition. I am sure it is you, David Anthony, I know you then and now.

David Anthony: Yes, me, My Dear Lady. My dearly essential one! I still want matter around me again. Then I note how souls behave in animalistic manners! Their reason is Hunger. For many things, they're unfulfilled and there's harsh elements! A need has grown for wanting to be noticed! Our ministry here, let's see... We just saw Rhetta and Mr. Marcher. Ugh, the disparity. He knows what he is doing.

My Lady: Yes, moving on with conscious over soul will of creator. About that jeep and mansion, one positions themself, playing games. Not spiritual.

Anthony: Haven't noted beings in other earth type planets conduct with pretense. Such a desire here to "outshine" as some put it! A story we'll learn. I am learning and glad to know you got through hard years back then, My Lady. My Dear One, I know how you lost so many so suddenly.

My Lady: Back on my feet, so to speak, am centered, I went through much self-correction, too.

Both David Anthony and My Lady: Time now to hop back in time, where the spacetime is March 2020, what had occurred eight months before Rhetta and Robert Marcher met.

Jumping Backward to March 13, 2020

(to where the Real Beginning is, of This Story)

Now he wants to know about…what? *'Various global studies defining and locating symptoms of narcissism: …individuals, groups. Mostly leaders, family order, intelligence, 1930 - on showing changes/growth.'* Then adds in his email *'with graphics corroborating data.'*

Mary laughed. It was over-used, this term. Wasn't 'self-esteem' also mentioned too much during her freshman year in college, eight or nine years ago? 'Narcissism' was trending too fast and most people didn't know the clinical definition, only some word to slam someone who seemed too assured, someone they didn't like.

Really now? Disorders created a need for academia to find and study and teach? Librarians to learn how to locate a department head's request because society is detecting the narcies? Why? Bloggers, chroniclers, pseudo shrinks warn!

Further reading revealed her grasp on this was very weak. Dr. Michael Merrick's sidenote, *then send to Foundation Library's sister scholarly groups, incl. focusses on evidence based.'*

Sociology courses years ago didn't hot-topic this term! She set his note aside with hope to convince the higher ups how his expectations were not listed in her faculty librarian contract.

Her Master's was 'history of cataloguing and circulation.'

Not a research librarian. The two recently departed Irma and Bess were. In December, they'd golden-hand-shook, then fled from this expressed chaos. Mary was now the only full-time faculty librarian. There used to be three of them.

Need back that self-esteem! Shake this compliance and malleability before lack-of-enthusiasm is arrested by guilt tripping.

She'd reached tenure last November. Instead of waving a 'congratulate me' flag, or sending announcements to nobody who'd care, she was phoning for help from the sister foundation college interlibrary forum -- and harnessing urges to not show her pathetic poise. She was swamped. Unfairly so.

The college's main student library was housed across the quad. Years before, faculty librarians requested remote labs and offices where Mary set up her desk. Student and hourly staff, she'd heard recently, were calling in ill. Yesterday, faculty part timers and a lab tech reported fever; two assistants visited urgent care.

The phone rang; it was Professor Merrick. Letting it go to voicemail was okay. She'd seek narcissism queries in hard journals first. The chocolate was making this bearable.

But her feet, for the third time this month, completely went numb. This was due to the juvenile habit of sitting on them. It cut circulation. About to jaunt toward behavioral hardback journals. She attempted to stand.

She was sorry.

Pins and needles prickled throughout her legs and numbed feet. She lost bearing. The wall in her front view swooped vertically as she smacked down. A slapstick no one was around to see. Bess and Irma would be offering hands. But today there were no witnesses. She struggled, got up, shook both feet.

It's the new culprit, that chocolate surge. Blame now would be allocated toward her morning's discovery behind the microwave, a motherlode of candy boxes. *It is your caffeine intake, sugar addiction that causes one to move too fast, unthinkingly.*

8

The dive dizzied her. Prickles stayed. She knew not to try online indexes. Wrestling the system would be a waste of time because of miserable failings, several times daily.

For weeks data indexes had increasingly failed to surface or would show for a second and too soon flunk off. She headed toward the Social Psychology cabinet. Over there! Load up on personality disorder reports. But first....

Fetch your Squib Book.

The Squib Book was the self-invention she'd used daily to preserve her sanity.

Ignoring the thrice ringing phone, she ran back to her desk, hugging ten, then back to the stacks again to pull the newest published reports with narcissism study results. But her desire borrowed her work ethic a minute here and there every day. Her 'March 2020' Squib 'issue' beckoned. Draft its raw form -- she pushed the journals temporarily aside. *'Catch juicy fresh muse meat before the chef edits.'*

This was *her* structuring motto.

She wrote, '... *stigma tag of 'narcissism', definition published in 1800, defined psychological terms, Feb 2020 distortions by self-proclaimed experts (like bloggers, pseudo scholars). Today there's much interest in this And I want to say that I'm not a narcissus, but maybe I am. Dunno yet.*

Moments after the December retirement party for Bess and Irma, Mary had squib-recorded about it. The two often turned the comedy on whenever finding personality disorder topics – how a trace of one showed up in themselves -- from depression, anxiety, to nervous eating to multiple personalities.

Mary had quickly then squibbed how, while in that day's

9

gleeful celebration, the two chewed chocolate and sang, "*love me self the most, kiss best upon myself, Bye now, I retire now, you and I must love we selves.*" They'd giggled and swayed like schoolgirls.

Keeping Squib Books hidden was wise, it was her recreation. An office hour 'borrowed' (fast scrawling) justified even more hours grading papers -- at home. She taught two 'History of Libraries' on-line classes, that was part of her contract and began to code so not to get busted.

Squib monthlies documented administration's lackadaisicalness. Job-post stalling for two research librarian replacements was high. '*Idiots would be in hot water if no faculty existed to teach 'Library Research Techs' by autumn semester.*'

All disciplines from Art to Kinesiology wanted librarians' time. All grew more difficult wrestling cyber issues The breakdowns during deadlines reminded Mary of her waitressing days when busloads of hungry tourists poured in as the stoves died. Then they'd run out of cream.

Behavioral Sciences Department's requested research needs outweighed other departments. Professor Dr. Michael Merrick's directive, usually, while in steep phases of first and secondary research, had overloaded research librarians. Besides teaching, he specialized in study building, mostly within his group of sister library scholars.

According to Bess and Irma, his topic demands were arbitrarily chosen. Ever-growing data had originally been installed archaically fifteen years ago. More meta space wasn't a salve. They'd employed dinosaur discovery layers to search and find. Any navigation instructions? Bess and Irma had left none.

Open-source conflicts were now causing a facial muscles twitch. Walking past the wall mirror, she glimpsed at the reflection of her head shaking "no" and her eyes praying "post positions!" Any smeared chocolate or new blemishes? *Is that an example of narcissism? Of course not. Then, why do I need a mirror? More so, why care how I look here? Not a soul besides and I'm not a model.*

'*Why is 2020 crippled with a degraded system? This, in the era of higher education?*' She squibbed dryly. '*Anyone care about me here?*'

Topping it, no person congratulated her when attaining tenured level. No spouse, no boyfriend, and Meghan, her daughter, at age eight, wasn't processing this news.

The janitor had a scoop. An administrator was admitted into the hospital, and three part-time assistants called in with the same type of virus symptoms making the world news.

Daily her work list grew. She checked off done ones quickly and began to slam her feet on the floor. Sitting on them was unallowed since the trip and fall. But candy was okay.

Oh, delicious! Now into her fourth nuttier, chunkier salted chocolatey sweetness, she stopped, stunned at the computer screen, spotting a message monster.

In the email queue. **She saw RED.**

A burst. Real heat began. A screaming, fat email directive.

Boldened letters. Collegewide: **Very Important**! In red. LED phone lights joined the drama. Professor Dr. Michael Merrick's name popped up. Placing him on hold so she could read the administration email, it cited W.H.O. showed the virus as extreme. A PANDEMIC. Written orders were huge.

'**LOCK DOWN. ALL SECTIONS IMMEDIATELY SWITCH TO ON-LINE ONLY.**'

Mary spewed her chocolate concoction. Nutty brown splashed onto the screen's glass, obscuring print, then boomeranged in splats on her blouse, then the keyboard.

Bitterness streamed her nasal cavity. Coughing. Snorting.

She released his hold. "Hello Doctor. Excuse me while I wipe off the screen!"

"Mary... so you *are* answering – and you're *coughing?*"

"It's a choke. Listen, I am the only person here! Saw you've sent emails, and I haven't opened any yet."

"You didn't finish my request from yesterday?"

It was eight a.m. "Professor, you must be or should be reading the urgent one from the administration."

Now a longer pause than usual, likely his recognition of her rank transgression. But carefully, he asked if she had a cold or felt head achy. *No. Do stop letting him chat*, she was thinking *he'd already taken up too much of my time.* "I am alright. I need to go. I've retrieved some reports."

At once, dozens of reply-to-all's burst out, ragging nonstop. Campus-wide, workers behind their computers pontificating stupid 'leadership' moves.

Her chuckle reverberated. Who here ever does anything quickly? Getting ready to learn what to endure. Re-format face-to-face to online? Syllabi were distributed months ago! Crazy!

The campus rocked, freshest emails highlighted latent issues. She equated the head's attention shifted from job posting. She would step on the gas to chase it harder.

A senior technician blasted a note: "Stop all your Reply-Alling! It's beyond *annoying*. Go rent a room to steam off passion. Grow up!" People began searching online for masks.

Buzzing phone, Merrick again. She picked the phone up and skipped the polite greeting. "With orders for doors to stay locked, there will be *no* library traffic. Professor, I will say again, I'm without essential librarians and without support staff!"

"Mary, then, I'd like every data index password and the ones to every discovery layer that you have been using. That saves us time." Both knew that was against the rules.

'*Learn more joy in work,*' she later squibbed. '*This too will pass.*' She mustn't fool herself these next days.

Merrick, five minutes later: "try finding the newly arrived bundle trial offers, my soc-psych journals! Credit is to be sent."

'*Oh, so he thought she was the main accountant for the library, too*'.

"Still, Mary, so not to bother you much, please, soon provide me passcodes, and old bibliographic data based ones."

She called the V.P. offices.

"Retirees left me loads of questions," without using the word 'messes,' "Please, can you tell me the date, when the job announcements are to be posted?"

The VP staff gave indefinite, non-answers on job posts, then a firm "no" on password sharing. This was likely due to a nebulous mandate after someone misused privilege.

'*Virus from another country, disappear, like a miracle, go away!*'

Her squib got nasty. Then she dialed Meghan's sitter, Gracie, whose college-prepping babysitting purse welcomed. Mary texted Meghan: '*I promise picnic Saturday xox! Gracie tonight! Leftover stew. Lock doors. Wash hands.*'

When would she remind Merrick about attaining tenure? Or if he remembered she had been a former student? This too presumptuous? She admitted desire to be highly revered.

Was this or would this be considered narcissistic?

'Missing link prospects' and *'Dr. In-Absolute'* were squibbed labels she'd secretly tagged on him while he'd been her professor, years before she was hired. He divided his attention too much, according to her. Getting a master's degree hadn't been her plan during those years. Her fiancé, Dr. Anthony, was a part-time chemistry instructor there.

It wasn't until mothering a bright, growing daughter alone and being receptive to benefits of earning a higher degree. Social psychology over-expanded – then. **But cataloging fitted her.**

And now she was forced into research

In One of Their Homes, the Marchers
April 1, 2020

The mailman loved the Marchers. Seeing them a few times a year, at this one home of theirs, was a treat. Today he handed her a letter from Rhetta Bandy and she set it down after a second's peruse. Dena once told Joseph she was Rudy's 'senora,' having met him while employed as an administrator at a community college. There, she'd noted his brilliance.

The mailman was not a great student. He looked at Rudy like a God, in awe. Rudy imagined algebraically, rarely sought a pencil to solve problems, and solved circles around most. And, strangely, Rudy drifted along silently, nearly invisibly within learning disability groups - being evaluated as borderline autistic and nearly retarded.

14

"He had rarely studied. He'd only focused wherever his current desires were," Dena, in warming tones, pointed out, while remembering to ask about Joseph's family and children. Beyond Joseph, she shared with everyone how her total awe of finding an 18-year-old who tracked progression of everyone instead of copying other's answers.

And this was a time when "technology" was overawing, others were stumbling, Marcher was a hidden goldmine "I'd plucked from the pity nest! Thus, individualized, up-to-date, and comprehensive lessons with the top counselors – some gladly traveled from other districts just to simply get a glimpse of the learning-disabled learner geek."

She took a breath, smiled, and added, "who was also very charming and handsome."

His self-confidence grew under her caring, hawk-eyed supervision. Being eleven years older, she felt maternal privilege. She proposed. There was no counter.

But today, in their Virgin Island home, it was dawning that their three kids were transforming into snots. Already they learned the skills of economic leveraging to benefit themselves *only* - anywhere. Annella, Ned, and Liam were also endowed like royalty, plus with good looks.

Now while opening Rhetta's envelope, she noted the femininity, uniqueness in stationery, and lovely handwriting. She read quickly, as she would any business document.

"Rudy, Rudolfy, Deary, Deer Doe Fawny!" Dena would comically growl chained endearments some days or be sweet like a little princess kitten. "Do you remember a girl named Kelli from high school having a sister, named Rhetta? Seems Kelli passed." She wondered how much effort to exert here? "How to precisely scent out? Love or the hunt for money. Or both?"

Someone inquiring how to effortlessly fall into the arms of Dumb Luck Land? Maybe reuniting with good 'old becoming friends-on-the-heels-of-my sister, sister Kelli? Who is that?"

"My first girlfriend." He looked off, far away. "She died?"

Dena read more of the letter for herself, then out loud. She saw his eyes becoming enamored in a memory.

"Let's do our usual. I never met her. I can't predict. Greet to treat or defeat – or not, you figure. And how." Rudy offered.

Rudolf didn't recall Kelli having a sister nor had heard the name Rhetta. How very sad if the dear girl had died! His memory told him enough, but he'd rarely thought about her since Dena.

Rudy's eyes, they always told her. He'd learned to filter raw honesty for the sake of others' feelings. His 'borderline autistic' wandering syndrome was highly specialized, aimed treatment privately referred as 'the musing outer space gaze.'

He was more pronounced in few emotional areas and underdeveloped in others. Always a surprise, a crap shot of how he'd behave. His mental capacity transfixed them.

"I haven't thought about her much since you, Dena."

"Again! The fawning," she laughed, teasingly. The oft used word was history with them. It referred to the 'F' word and their collection of deer art and literature. She'd selectively share how when their children were small, that 'fawning' substituted vulgarity. 'Fawn this' or 'Fawn it' or 'Fawn off' usage replaced the 'F' word usage when their children heard much, understood more, and were learning to talk.

"Yes, be fawned within by your own feats, dear deer!"

Rudolf read Rhetta's letter – three times. Slightly amused

16

but each time he was a bit more impressed.

"Delve dive first and/or prepare proper footwork?"

"Prior to more mail, a call, or meeting her?" "Two to four months of delving" "Get Don Creed on it."

Kelli's death was stunning, yes, a harsh reminder of lifetimes flown by fast and he remembered he'd been sad when they'd been split up so suddenly by her parents.

He realized his moods were jumping around, reeling from Dena's earlier suggestion, he'd self-axed political hedge funding ties. Both the politic-pandemic and prognosis of Dena's illness gnawed him. All noticed how much Dena had slowed but adamantly refused to ingest pain aids. This pierced her pain threshold which in turn exacerbated combativeness at times.

On every decision she insisted she'd be the only negotiator and signer of world business and family trust. Big money came after being married only ten years; solid consultation from specialists and lawyers had not been easy.

Educating Rudy on social mores made only minimal sense to him. He'd laugh at most culturally accepted behaviors. He'd ignore being told he should think or feel a certain way – He deeply depended on his own private logical sense.

Rudolf trusted her explicitly. She explained all well to him - social taboos, body language, reasons for staying silent instead of blurting what might be embarrassing. However, he stuck to being loyal to himself, blurting more appropriately.

The sunset over the canal cast peaches and pinkish pastels upon his face, complementing the sweet tanginess of her iced tea. He was still so handsome, more so each year. He sparked energy and love in and from her. Dena, with her illness, weighed much these days, her children's future, her soul's journey, family legacy.

Had he recently imagined being single widower? Yes, she relented, this was logical. Her ailment would spur even a saint to plan. And yes, it stung. Her smart, innocent, snatched-up student/boy missed out on an entitled normal 'thirties' stages.

Would hot gold-digging women with incredible prowess start in on him? Swarm in too quickly - for him? "'Just hand over the money if you really care, Rudolf,' that's what they'd say, do, and act like, Rudy," she'd already lightly, lovingly warned him of the possibility. He swore no woman interested him.

The truth, and he knew it, was he couldn't function without her. Maintaining secrecy about her ailment was her directive, to be shared between only the two of them, but twice, her tiredness prompted two kids to question if she'd been tested for the virus.

"ALL are going on that cruise," his words were Dena's prompt. "Medics to join us!" It would be on their favorite yacht, a renovated *The Fallow*, to arrive through the locks, newly tuned.

His goal, early in their marriage, was grabbing chances to be with his four cats wrapped around his neck while studying. With Dena's push, he was renowned computer software scientist.

Striking gold, best companies sought a breadth of skills. Getting his PhD was not difficult, and the Marcher's received widely known recognition. He knew how to advance. In 2001 co-owned companies were sold; new billionaires suddenly appeared.

He again read the letter. Together they'd battled droves of shady ones enchanted with gaining money for nothing.

Dena probably was on this, right now, instructing one of their secretaries to gather the Rhetta's profile. Most importantly what suggestions are researched for the better future.

The Junipers, April 2020

It was her voice, her delivery. He knew her true key, wrong sharps and flats fogged intent and meaning - even to herself, especially after drinking and playing. Lately, he avoided confrontations brought by her anxiety or self-doubt, as he'd find himself tiptoeing on eggshells while encouraging better from her.

Both okayed forced isolation — separation brought relief. By April, in central Washington by dusk, they found themselves in separate areas of their mobile home. Online games and side-bar chat rooms intrigued all shut-ins. Mystery contenders were more fun than soaps, game shows or reruns! The activity was free.

Her 'Princess JJ' avatar guarded her, driving hormones, as did Jude's 'Dodge Bait.' He dodged reaction, then resumed baiting. And again, dodging them whenever girl avatars took bait. See the game? Self-fulfilling thrills played nightly, *hunting new, wasting time, but too bad, I'm drunk, it's what I do best.*

All masked "avatars" helped keep personal privacy, expressing anything in incognito. From bawdy flirting to rancor.

Goof-off-lock-down modes reigned. Janna drank her supper in white wine. Jude drank beer and munched cheese on popcorn. Keyboards became sticky. Nothing mattered in perfect privacy. Players ranged in skill, aced word games — failed bomb traps and tile builds.

Wary of avatars who just might be past girlfriends in disguise, (especially during word games) Jude's Dodgebait avatar stopped playing with them. He knew he was paranoid and drunk.

19

Furniture in the dark gave them toe jams while stumbling to bed. Startled yelping, as though being fooled. *Ouch, oh, how rude to take advantage of my drunken walk!* Their every morning hangovers were a small price; they didn't have to drive to work.

Most days, while Janna beautified her girlfriends, she enforced rules as her fingers combed and cut their hair, glammed nails or make-up. She would insert a sentence to cut off unnecessary romance tangle chats, complaints, exploits. "Next time don't knock until contacting me first, I won't be awake until 11 a.m. and won't answer." Whenever they stayed over to chat after they'd paid, Janna interrupted conversations with, "I will talk when I see you next Tuesday, good day now!"

Jude could barely maintain his scrap art business since art was now classified as a 'nonessential' like other convenience or disposable products. He stored anything that might bend the right way, or entice a future work of art. He labeled it as recycled art. He'd be ready when art lovers returned to buy it.

One Friday an innovative '***Meet Gamer Mystery Friends!***' flyer promo to 'Gather unmasked online gamers! Be vaccinated!' This entity saw profit in lonely hearts who loved playing games all night, holed up in the dark. Gather them! Janna's and Jude's now mirrored gleefulness.

One would be held in August in the PNW! Close by! Meeting them de-costumed, un-avatar - a treat! All ordered to bring pandemic guards if covid hadn't left by then, miraculously.

LUMINSTRATUM

Rays play with cloudiness around David Anthony and My Lady. He refers to her more as "My Dear" as she resembles a past personality - in millions of years when they both were matter.

20

David Anthony: My Dear Lady, you report on seeing volatility!
    see, (he checks his unbiased processor). Will we intervene?

My Lady: Yes. Be close, near them. Units are 365 per
    cycle here

David Anthony: All these personalities we see here in the
    present are nearing onsets of huge change, but difficult to
    move through it all if they hold on to solitary self-
    importances, fighting to count, to be noticed, to be mattered.
    Now a pandemic. Later a factoring of faith and/or belief!

David Anthony: Celestials share stories after ministering
    earth types in other galaxies. To outshine is prevalent, I've
    learned. Tactics and motivations differ, though.

    How about Dena, a bias there? I love her philanthropy. Many
    reactions have puzzled me, like exactly what they'll really
    need from us. Since I have lapsed time in revisiting.
    Luminstrata – my own - is quickly getting stretched!

My Lady: You know, we've been celestial for more than
    ten years, David Anthony! I learned from other celestial
    spirits, all their tales. Variables and aspects!

    Neither can I get used to our existence without a body.

            (My Lady laughs, he goes on)

David Anthony: Did I know you when you did.

My Lady: Did what?

David Anthony: When having matter. A body.

My Lady: Same city we lived in, you can't recall now?

David Anthony: Difficult for me to count. I couldn't keep
    track, actually! That was then, My Lady. Dear, dear one. I've
    barely learned my lessons, and now still improving my
    outlook. I suppose I am celestially loving enough. Okay now.

21

And am now with you and with the will of the overseer.

My Lady:　　　　*Have you, like myself, been referred to as anything like a Spirit, Angel, Ghost, Morontial mota, spark speed, Guide, Spook, Sentinel, A Sign, Messenger being?*

David Anthony:　　　*Affirmative! Add more to what you said. A huge variety of cultures on many planets in this universe. Exponentially! Spirit definitions along with their synonyms. Some beings feel we're with them, as enlightened aides –*

My Lady:　　　　*That's fitting. Labels differ in each culture, in each experience – I find uniqueness in all of them. As with similarities in their common quest for the truth and the light..*

My Lady:　　　　*Tons of literature on this planet to select from. Regarded by non-believers to be fairy tales.*

David Anthony:　　　*Realized that truth, my Dear Lady Agent, co-attendant! We're to speed back and forth here in time.*

College Scholars April 2020

Country scholars considered the gathered studies of Dr. Merrick to be top notch, he was a truly fine social psychologist, excellent study planner, builder. Intuitive instructor.

Quick conclusions brought quick and numerous red flags. Rarely did any study smoothly receive a speedy total thumbs' up while in peer-review mode, and re-studies were summoned. New plan builds, calls for alterations, newer variables – for secondary data. Results from similar studies elsewhere.

'Missing links spurred redesigning. All discoveries and clarifying findings were shared within the PNW Sister Colleges Foundation Merrick spearheaded years ago. Data compiled fast.

Mike noted Mary could be better if she slightly displayed

glimmer of interest in Bess's and Irma's tasks. Inquiring with enthusiasm should replace freneticism. Yes, cyber issues clouded her progress, although and yet she found time to hint about her newly tenured status - which didn't matter to him.

He told her kindly 'her new self-perception' wasn't calling for celebration…*he'd be cheering when receiving his data.*

'Well, time to attempt observable interest.' She sensed he saw a treadmilling hamster. He was blocking the reality of brokenness. Pretending interest wasn't of her; it was time to tackle the truth.

His plate was very full, her plate full, broken and ignored.

Thursday, while phoning, he'd asked if she'd been tested for Covid She'd sounded stuffy, her words came out sluggish.

"I'm fine."

But how could she or anyone be certain? No reliable testing system had yet been implemented. Nursing homes reported more positively tested patients, then more outbreaks. More dying patients. All mandated to begin quarantining.

More chose to work from home.

Self-vowing he'd not share his opinion about politics because the circus misunderstood and relayed stupidity. People wanted to yell, not listen. His own path wasn't politics and power. It was to gain data, test to show results and factual truth.

Typical television cable and network propagated bias confirmation. Everyone had clueless pals pushing biased belief. Pulling in profit, greedy moguls gained a bigger audience.

The world was changing quickly by this pandemic. Too few attitudes were enlightened while learning. Subcultures shifted status quos and odd behaviors like stupid outrage and stubbornness reigned.

It was late, and Merrick swam in doctoral committee requests, syllabi revisions, and sabbatical plans. Mary hadn't yet sent requested journal articles. Irma had spoiled him.

Recalling desperation in Mary's voice began tugging his gut.

She wasn't treated fairly. Its dawning tweaked guilt. His baseball bulletin-board above stacked shoe-boxes full of 5" x 7" index cards, and decades of stats pulled his focus and concern.

 He opened one unused pack.

He decided to dedicate the blank ones to list issues she'd voiced. Heck, he'd spearheaded the Sister College Library Foundation, but turned deaf to her requests? His mother was saying *Shame, Mike* from wherever on the other side. He smiled.

The index card habit began in fifth grade and his fascination with the greats wouldn't leave him. No PC's then. His stats piled in stacked shoeboxes, data galore, handwritten.

On these, he'd list every library issue.

Call her? No. Through his dusty window, a lit campus shadowed the library with eucalyptus. Was she working late? It was past dinner time. Do his kids want rice and chicken tonight?

This coming August, he would kennel them, then drive his newly finished custom-built van to a wonderfully plush solitary spot. Camp alone, then later join study profs. Perfect reception needed, not to miss one baseball game! Newest scholarly data, or credible news? The sabbatical would last through November.

LUMINSTRATUM

A background of new atmospheric ambiance for David Anthony and My Lady continued to clearly be understanding each other.

David Anthony: My Dear Lady? Are you feeling something?

My Lady: Your tone is ... exactly what?

(My Lady laughs, he goes on)

David Anthony: How can nostalgia occur in me as a feeling, what is happening? I wish it was possible to phone a real lady for her thoughts, hold in my hand a receiver, hear her soft voice. Touch her with my hands. We're without good old telephones, like in the earthly good old-having-a-body days.

My Lady: Having trouble connecting? Need more curriculum training?

David Anthony: More lessons when this assignment ends, don't question the will of the highest.

My Lady: HOLD your guardian self, and I won't ask which lady. Dear David Anthony, are you operating slightly off assignment? You sideways? As they say, "Off the clock?"

I'm telling you I am informed of your past earth history.

David Anthony: Past history? How, and which?

My Lady: Know, David Anthony, that other earth-like planets aren't as obsessed with the physical act of progenerating! Many in other universes corrected by improving their planning. Purported as so.

David Anthony: Oh, next you'll say, 'Need I report you'.

My Lady: I don't report to or of you, I report to another.

David Anthony: Roger, My Dear Lady, I am curious with
    absolute care about what matters with everyone.

    Psychology of mattering (being noticed and its extremities).

My Lady: These report findings while they adapt to a
    pandemic - so utterly avoidable, as a sidebar, I will add.

David Anthoney: Am ordered to stop my former Anthony
nonsense! I misunderstood while at Sunday School.

Years ago, Professor Mike Merrick, PhD, mastered the art
of fixating 120 online students. He'd optimize a collective grasp
of his lessons, first, by imagining befriending the camera's lens as
his sole likeable, brilliant, attention-deficient learner.

All his taped lectures for fifteen years rested on his shelf
near his baseball table. Many were catalogued at the library. He
explored socioeconomics - education, race, gender, belief systems
-- as attitudinal variables, his unbiased delivery gave light.

Other professors taught online but not as well. Stumbles were
felt by students who'd exchange tips on-screen survival 'appear
engaged,' 'sport tinted large glasses,' – all to avoid receiving
absence marks! Most didn't get caught playing online games,
emailing, or social media via the underground buzz.

Eldest faculty fought 'ivory tower discontentment' and
were not morphing. It shook them, especially when younger staff
whispered about them. "They're lost when lecturing without
helms, grandfathered resisters are forced to live the real life!"
Mocking beneath the mask, "the hoax is for real!"

Reproached on rudeness, advisement was to acclimate.
Remediate: "Yes, Professor! Will do!" Earn that 'kissy rump'
annual review, "you're wise, prof, I'll explain again if you want."

More staff, students, and chancellors tested positive, some hospitalized, national death rates rose. Fighting ensued. Retirement queries grated HR's reiteration of accrued benefits.

Chapter TWO

Mary took personal need off for Monday, because Gracie's mom, Shari Land, tested positive for the virus. Not fully prepared to manage those two young females. Dawning now, she'd mismanaged a major parental responsibility.

It arose to bite on Sunday night.

"The picture of the man, is that him?" Gracie asked Mary, who busily graded quizzes. "Meghan asked just now about my dad. Then I asked her the same about her dad. Said she didn't know. I asked about the wall photo. She changed the subject."

Still, all was too tough to speak about Meghan's father. The short time between him and her, after he lost his chemistry adjunct position, was due to his unorthodox behavior.

Mary decided nothing to Meghan about Dave for now beyond he had departed. Mary saw Meghan still gazing at his portrait. It was time to divert. Teach them topics!

Show them how to venture into data whenever curious. Teach the two how to research! An activity assignment she used for her students was called "A Beautiful Question." Academic search databases (newspaper and journal articles on all subject areas) taught navigation skills.

She'd introduce opposing viewpoints' collections and uncover indexes. Help them clarify. Look for the right questions.

For Meghan and Sitter (likely dear Gracie)

RESEARCH using our study room computer. Find my bibliographic folder files and then search the "Your Unique Question" assignment listed below. I have a word to start with. Then think of yourself after the first day's assignment. First start with:

1. Beliefs. Ask yourself how do beliefs differ with everyone? What are your personal questions once you understand definitions? Feel free to include Deity and/ or Creator. How about compare it with "Faith." You will come across more you'll want to understand. Daily, fill your assignment with YOUR new word to investigate, YOURS which opened your curiosity.

(if you have questions, ask me before summer begins!) Love you, Mom

PS *Always ask what, where, why, how, and when.* And a note to herself wrote: *Soon talk about Dave.*

Tuesday morning, the second she saw her desk she felt the oddness. Activity occurred during her long weekend absence. Without immediate visual evidence, she was certain. Odd, yes. She opened her email. Aunt Madeline was inquiring about the August family reunion. Mary hadn't yet made solid plans.

To avoid committing, her response described current problems in the library, saying she'd update them in a few weeks.

Then, like a dream, the echoing of Irma's and Bess's bubbly laughter bellowed, and their familiar down-step gaits grew louder. They appeared, wearing masks, getting closer.

It's them! Five months of retirement, then out of the blue, why bustle in? Instant memories of a mal-functioned family gathering surfaced. Always, one relative would eagerly join with genuine gleefulness, a 'glad to see you all,' but too soon all waned into an intrusive mission of gaining information just to pass on.

Mary quickly smoothed her mask, glad to cover her mouth which didn't have a welcoming smile. She'd wrestled problems they'd left. Also, there might be chocolate on her teeth.

"Hey Girlie Girl, haven't turned on your research database oldies and goodies yet? Missed you yesterday and Sunday…oh, and Saturday! Mike brought four people fixing and replacing!

"New magic for the faculty library!"

Bess pointed toward the lab. "New computers for graduate students! When you key in, notice a smoother ride! New layers! Gremlins stepped up to the saving of the library! Kudos to us!"

Irma said, "Hurray. Give me a hug, Girlie Girl!"

Mary was reeling like in a dream. *'Hey,'* she squibbed later, *'a salve poured over this place, the networks soaking in it, every former flunking hardware, cloud, and data retrieval kink has been cured! There is much newness! Subscriptions installed perfectly; It's almost like Christmas!*

"Each subscription has its own password, adhering to the college's nebulous rules. Here's a list!" Bess firmly slapped the service contract receipt in Mary's hands.

Mike jubilantly joined and read her expression. "The VP gave me a key, and I'll return it after tweaking for details." His 'fix-it-all' urgent requisition from IT had been met after VP heads sped up permissions from the foundation.

Mary caught herself sitting on her feet again. She placed them back on the floor and spotted dog toys and a cat brush under her desk – with a half-eaten dried biscuit.

Irma bubbled, "We've been travelling since January! I understand you were abandoned without a clue of the sticky navigation bumps. Got so bad for you!"

Mike added, "I'm instructed to tell you to change all passwords. Keep them secret!" He smiled as though pleasing his family. "A piece of chocolate, please.! I smell the coffee already!"

Two weeks later, Mary still worked overtime to complete daily predicaments. No Research Librarian post. The Sister College library was crowded with secondary research. Mike's spearheading and his department loaded both sets of librarians.

Nothing in the next weeks between she and Mike changed professionally or personally. She stayed spiteful, still talking via email. She'd dreamt of an aura framed his face. His pets and students followed him distributing sociology logoed masks.

"Do you have kids, pets? My kids are spoiled. They get piped music and heated floors," he shared with students and other faculty, trying to lighten glumness all around the campus.

Many agreed Mike had odd characteristics. He rode a bike to work, wore no socks, talked while biting straws, and would rapidly redirect conversations whenever boundaries were crept upon. He caught drifts quickly and illuminated with dry humor.

Minutes each day, Mary wiped covers, cleaning germs - off the collection of faculty textbooks. The current Social Psychology 301 differed from three years ago. The Table of Contents listed new topics: Gender Identification, Growth of Agnosticism, plus Socioeconomics Affecting Status of Women.

Her eyes caught the author on the archived textbooks. Dave's. Dave, when with her for the several years taught astronomy and chemistry there, part time.

Her throat swelled. Why did remembering or being reminded by his name strike a nerve? By 2020, she'd thought it would have faded, not be full of punctuated emotion.

The quad clock struck ten p.m. After a take-out dinner, Mike had returned to compose an email, reiterating he'd be away August through December 2020, for an already scheduled sabbatical. He also noticed Mary's light was on.

'Also', he added, *'…continue to pay attention to the library's recent implementation; we've elevated in value. The Foundation needs additional donations to fund other areas. Thousands will benefit. And most important, during my absence this library __must__ have recruited new research librarians.'*

Mary, driving home, knew in her tired bones how she needed a break from all of this. She imagined joining the 3-day family reunion come August even while acknowledging it could become Covid cancelled, but she must use her vacation time!

Junipers are Pumped Up

People remained dependent on news through familiar comfort zones confirming biases, unable to be convinced by any hint of an opposing viewpoint. The media polarized. Broadcast and cable moguls depended on malleable audiences.

It seemed to Mary that people liked fighting. And staying misinformed. Confirming their own biases.

This didn't stop people from wanting to party. Up north with the Junipers, "Beneath the Avatar Weekend Meet-up" was in fast-paced set-up mode, even though other venues throughout the nation cancelled due to ordinance protocols.

Their nearest meetup was located 27 miles away! Faces began smiling, liking the idea, *"let's do the copter! Yes!"*

Jude's pre-pandemic passed piloting test was helpful. They'd save travel money. Senior Juniper had died two years before, bequeathing a kit-built copter. For months it sat rusting, still on a friend's car lot. Inheritance would help a lot!

Several mobile home neighbors despised the Junipers. "They'd voted for the bad party." Newly coiffed unmasked ladies walked near neighbors' windows, checking reflections, blowing spit-filled air on newly painted nails. Nasty 'anonymous' notes soon got tucked under Juniper's doormats and windshield wipers.

'Beyoo-ti-shun! MaskUP - Vote Better Next Time!'

It didn't bother Janna. The thought of seeing whites of player pals' eyes brought fantasy. Would BAWMU be attended by so-and-so, you know, the Jet Guy who jokes and cheats in word games? Or "Charlie's Lucy" who swears using grawlixes?

'Play board games!' Bulletins added, *'Wipes will be provided. Covid safety guidelines will be adhered to. Price $450 apiece! Food included.'*

"There is a God!" Jude shouted, he waved certified mail from a lawyer managing his dad's estate, stating $15,679 would arrive by early August. They could pay off their credit cards!

Jude felt ecstatic because closed art fairs had stalled his sales and was failing to meet his overhead half. Though it was odd for the Junipers to agree quickly, they vowed this time to seal their lips; money was no one's business. He'd not mention his kids living with their mom. Janna's kids wouldn't ever hear it.

A bit of Nut-shelling Yachts and the Marchers

The "over entitled-little-know-it-alls" with uninhibited boredom meant never pretending pleasure for politeness. With minimal enthusiasm, they toasted parental success. Rudy announced it was time all be together to review the year's development status updates with about a plan for Dena's health – now, today, all full disclosure.

Liam wanted to hear about the nearly finished commuter airports in three corners of the country. Ned was drawn to his parents' clean energy investment dividends and investments. Annella focused on whatever her friends 'celebrated her' about.

Medics said "accept" that no ready trial treatment could guarantee Dena's improvement, "but do stay positive, one was aimed for completion within months."

She was highly aware medical care quality was widely unaffordable. Citizens were lucky if their employer offered it. At any time, her live-in nurses, each on twelve-hour shifts, were ready to fulfill demands. "My middle-class parents barely had basic comforts of having a quality doctor."

This, along with a decline in traditional two parent families having installed agreeable children to care for their aging parents. Aging boomers would be without willing support. Insurance would become more expensive without improving care quality.

When Marcher's family's fifth house located in Charlotte Amalie, a Virgin Island address, had two elevators, heated floors, and sculpted mahogany walls, Dena was slow to realize how non-essential objects were failing to make them truly happy.

Their spending, years ago, had been influenced by her kids' snide remarks, such as, "don't bother buying it unless it is the VERY BEST!" So, the family got the best. "Everyone expects us to have the best. Because we're super rich."

Well, Dena thought, *you've earned none of it all by yourselves, and I don't like this coming out of any of you!* She decided to say it to them.

And soon they would learn and receive a bigger reality check.

Her stomach was sickened the day she realized the weight of their expectations, seeing how just seconds after new items reached their hands they lost their luster, and a new smell disappeared when delivered to ungracious arms.

This contrasted Rudolf's avoidance to speak of frill effect, letting her handle issues. He preferred focusing on innovations but listened to her talk strategy with the kids' unwarranted, pompously assumed superiorities. They bullied. They took credit for ideas generated from less advantaged acquaintances.

33

Something in child rearing art and science was missed. She needed to be counseled on all this quickly.

Captain Halbert knew most about the kids, the *Fallow*, cuisine, the investor clubs, and how to throw great parties. He tutored the Marcher kids in their elementary years. Often, he'd surprise Dena with sparkling details he'd stored, like colors and food each liked, how each would react to something. Dena asked he start remembering tastes and preferences of the guests instead.

Their global excursions brought invitation to a sundry of diverse social affairs. This warranted armors of consultants and legal staff. Halbert knew when and how to gracefully step everything up while customizing games for guests. He loved discovering reactionary behavior, and after a fruitful year, the Marchers published '*The Halbert Angles bent by the Marchers*'.

The Halbert's cuisine and orchestration of yacht meetings drew in the famous, mega wealthy, some simply scholarly, but all "fawned out" on atmosphere whenever with the Marchers.

Studying each guest developed a party game called "build your dream boss" "dream neighborhood" "dream product" "dream care voyage for life and beyond." The Marchers paid close attention to how guests processed their thoughts, how they behaved, reacted, how they planned. This segued into specialized personal fun data collections, thus more formulated innovations.

Guests became potential investors and remained on the party list then later brought dates or mates who were consultants or capitalists. All would leave pumped up and grinning, challenged by innovativeness. Minds traveled fun obstacle courses – all loved Rudy Marcher, the brilliant oddity.

When in grade school, the Marcher kids couldn't read their dad well enough, especially when on excursions. He'd not laugh when the group laughed, nor show sadness or anxiety or anger.

Not much of Rudolf was understood by anyone other than Dena.

The Halbert's knew to translate their dad's behavior. Understandable logic that 'being special' meant simply 'he won't pretend emotion' – 'doesn't mean he's angry, likely he's smiling inside,' 'his eyes or his mouth won't show he is in his very own head party!' 'doesn't know to fake it!'

"We'll sign him up for acting classes, how's that? We know he likes to dance with a cane!"

Rudy was malleably willing to participate, surprisingly. Whatever Dena wanted. So, acting classes brought awareness in identifying people's facial expressions. By the time their real money entered in, he grasped what was happening in other people's faces. He became more 'with it' and chuckled more.

But he couldn't explain why something was funny. The fawning jokes started up, then, created by himself! The drama classes worked. 'At least appear as though you are more open and an engaging person. Practice in a mirror. Film it. Study your face!'

Business journals headlined successes. This led to meshing with political shakers. Dena brought continued challenges; he loved studying patterns of formation, movement, planning mechanics, and oh, logistics! An endless chess game.

Unknown to most, Dena had decided after one party that she would soon invite her probate team to go with her on the cruise once they were near reaching Santa Barbara. Re-write her plans so kids won't be able to blow any of it after she has passed.

May 2020, at the College

By late May, it became a habit to coordinate masking, laundering, and increased hand washing. Meghan sweetly accepted change.

A new early morning eagerness birthed in Mary; she began relishing what she hadn't, months prior. Deeper curiosity awoke inside of her. What info today would be needed by which department faculty member? She minimized coffee refills in the morning and corrected herself whenever accidentally sitting on her feet.   Reverence for library science processes involved teamwork in safekeeping databases. Humans forever, everywhere, need more catalogued storage within indexes.

On Monday Mike emailed Mary: *secular after-life belief systems (include range of atheists, agnostics. pantheists and non-disclosed) in the following countries...'* followed by *[list]* *'21ˢᵗ century persuasion/propaganda global sexism [compared to 1950's & on],'* then minutes later, *'more on gender identification 1850 to 1950,'*

"Could two of these unrelatable requests perhaps be delegated to sister colleges? Forwarded to Utah?" Mary asked. His obliging to her request was shooting three more for her to handle, but knew she'd be quick – "giving you more practice."

"Just these three on narcissism in rural vs. metro, thanks, Mary. I see you've found much in this discipline."

She thought driving home. Again, the narcissism interest was constant. Why? Looks, smarts, arrogance? Expectation for attention? Entitlement over others? Hogging the spotlight?

Psychologists were writing more about nuances within dozens of types. There was malignant narcissism (antisocial traits), there was communal (inflated community image), and cerebral (intellectual superiority). Somatic, grandiose, and more.

All faculty conducted themselves with their own unique prominence, bearing professional personas while requesting research. Rare was casual chit chat whether from math, art, history, or economics. Specialty knowledge filled the room. She soaked in quotes of the great thinkers. She absorbed each of their passions. Fibonacci occupied her mind one week, Charles Horn, Michaelangelo, and Roosevelt, too.

When an astrophysicist of a chemistry archived study was brought to her attention by a woman PhD, she thought of Dave.

Before becoming an adjunct while earning his degree, Dave, her fiancé taught chemistry and astronomy in high school. He was great with slower learners. Those learners weren't handicapped. They paused more during processing. Elements in astronomy interested him. Although by 2019 when astrophysicists had found the element calcium in space, she knew he, Dave, would have associated the calcium in milk to the Milky Way for mnemonic purposes. Calcium is in dairy products!

But Dave was no longer, only remained a remnant.

Now to manage his effect on her, Dr. Merrick interpreted his drive. Three times in two days he began inserting friendlier tones in his notes: *Mary, your coffee still warm? Did you find published opinion elsewhere?*

Then, two days later, a different angle turn: *"Today I need different highway maps of the Pacific Northwest!"*

What? The Northwest highway maps? Hedging non-professional territory? He continued, *"by the way, my sabbatical begins August 2nd. Away fall semester! You're probably glad I'll be absent."*

Startled, yet invisibly smiling, she wouldn't be in concurrence. Her amiss gut translated shaky amusement. Tinges of insecurity mixing with romanticism? She didn't need or want this giddy mixed-up feeling. Past drama saw her tidying falsetto while planning to run from a likely future wound.

Wary and weary, she wanted to help other professors. One

in English, one in Art, one in kinesiology who wasn't pushy. She liked humility and smart consideration.

Each day his imagination designed details of a platinum white luxury van. Given this project more time, he changed the semester's finals. Students were instructed to design their finals. Grades would be based solely on quality of thought processes. One student, while handing in his final, saw Merrick push pinning van photos near the autographed baseball pictures.

Merrick added a quick P.S. to Mary, …"*not for Sosigh, today it's refrigerators, my self-designed van, Mary, it's nearly ready. I need help. It needs a fridge. Please search when you have time. Today. Please.*"

How calmly he'd thrust his needs at an open opportunity.

'*Dr. Merrick, you're asking for personal or professional?*' did not get asked, her stomach quivered, churned, she was losing footing. Caving into subordinance, her voice was getting lost. Without refute he received five van fridge hyperlinks within two hours.

Why am I so weak?

Wrestle again with the squibbing! It read. '*P.S: Do know definitions of hegemony, oh, also, senior entrenched tenure - known as 'Entitlement' which silences? It's wrong. Even if you saved the library!*'

Of course, not to share that, instead, she employed her library campus-wide department blog:

'*Thank you for understanding library rules! This pandemic challenges us, still, to remain courteous and professional. Few realize I am the only 100% on-site faculty librarian, barely managing three contract jobs and two online classes. Two part-time adjuncts work off campus. My one contract contains explicit functions. Let's provide best service to our students.*'

Mike's daily requests plunged, asking nothing of her for five entire days. Others asked at their usual pace, submitting requests on forms, as they were asked to do, from baroque artist comparisons to English poetry author biographies.

She knew Mike realized he'd been flagged, and he chose not to address her on this. It was quiet. She went home on time.

But too soon she caught herself checking emails more often for anything he may have sent to her. She glanced out the window, wondering why his shades were drawn. Maybe he was ill. On the fifth day she parked on a different lot, drove around it twice to check if his bike was parked with the other two wheelers.

By the end of day five, she was relieved. The mail trickling-ins of him, his words crawling like a punished child's, *"no great rush on this, Mary. But --"*

For the next week he remained in check.

And Mary stopped work by 7:00 p.m. instead of 10:30 p.m.

He resumed without personal salutations or over lengthy closings. But on Wednesday she saw an entirely new pitch. He kindly asked her for a past century European family culture study.

She would deeply regret how she chose to respond. Her entire body had grown to be invigorated by the sight of his name. Talking had not been her plan. She wrote to him: *"Europeans during that era? I'm absent early August. Likely, I will enjoy a PNW family reunion with many transplanted Europeans! Of course they'll be distancing. Not 1925 culture, but 2020 in the good old US at that!"* She re-looked again, after emailing. Chatted too much, caved. Stupid. She tried retracking it.

It was gone, in his territory. Her professional boundary. Gone. Big parts of last week's blog-craft plunged. All bent. Big time. By herself she'd built. She'd torn and reacted like a teen. Now what to do? Her veins pumped.

His too soon response popped: *"The reunion to be held where?"*

Against her best judgement, she replied exactly where it would be, then followed up by asking him where his site was located. He again quickly responded, then added *"new camp/study site! When exactly is your reunion? Am scheduled to set out August 2nd!"*

She caved again *"On the calendar for our family meet and greet!"*

It took Merrick two days to propose. He'd provide gasoline and meals while they'd share the drive. Inside his new luxury van, with him. On the way he suggested, she'd use her laptop to access more. Don't forget flash drives, all full ones! Newly bought ones!

He hadn't, though, arranged a stipend or planned to give credit toward her contributions, though. Or had he? An accessory passenger owned passwords to those precious subscriptions.

The platform was to be all his without asking about her needs or suggestions? Neither flew in to rescue and he sensed within days her growing hesitation. Passing through the quad area, behind the hygiene mask, her weary, apprehensive eyes tried diversion. She looked almost frightened of him.

He gently clarified: "A ten-hour, scenic drive, Mary. I'm eager to explore the indexes! Variants galore. Abstracts needed, bringing a list for our drive. I could really use more – like of the quality you've been recently supplying. Sabbatical needs it."

Oh, so bring her portable rechargeable printer? He wasn't monkeying around, "I assure you, Mary, I'm great at my job and know it is all I'm great at. I also understand how much I am **not** good at. The hours aren't to be considered as dating, Mary."

Then, "We have shared a rough semester."

She concluded he thought he wasn't good at whatever was the ex-factor. Endeared, enticed, and a tad embarrassed, though. Surprisingly, she looked forward to sharing the ride. Shyly, she asked later for compensation. Kudos to yourself, lady.

40

LUMINSTRATUM

Within the backdrop of mist, voices of David Anthony and My Lady.

David Anthony: What a handful, guarding. With all the words in many languages, people still cannot express themselves well to each other. In most cases. Is that ego or pride or wisdom?

My Lady: Depends. Mary is a single mother, a dear. We will learn more. Mike and she might get closer.

David Anthony: Yes, that is likely. There are sparks about something, not sure what, though. Others are lonely down there, even lonely while facing each other, sitting with each other, too, all wanting to matter, not sharing feelings.

David Anthony: Years ago I existed around there.

My Lady: Interesting, David. I was there only to see, not intervene, not share.

David Anthony: The Will has communicated. There's something for us to back burner focus on. Concerning elements, and the atoms which differ in certain areas there. Something mysterious about music and the construction of unknown instruments, A man is questioning his sanity at times, and rightly so. Concert? Metals?

My Lady: I hear it! The sounds intersect with my focus on love, philanthropy, and expression.

David Anthony: Give pleasure, share pleasure. Pleasure is as important elsewhere, everywhere, it appears! Ego seems to be widespread, though, or less covert, than I remember. Haven't seen this much effort for self-power in other planet worlds.

Janna and Jude finished overstuffing backpacks, four in all, and included were alcohol and snacks and Janna's cosmetics. Also, a few pastel boxes held many sketch pads. "Uh, don't forget the facemasks, although we won't use them."

"Pack more party favors!"

Hundreds of miles south of the Junipers, Hawkings and Merrick were already on the road. He, for a minimum of 16 weeks, and she, merely two evenings, were set to enjoy first their casual discourse. He changed into a sweet, chatty schoolboy.

Mary noted he looked at her differently. Whether it be admiration or investigative? physical, spiritual or intellectual?

Mary decided weeks ago to stay secret from colleagues and neighbors. Who had the right to details? Only slightly with Meg whose focus was summer camp - or whatever Gracie was wearing or listening to. All had each other's cell number.

Only one RSVP went to Mary's forgetful aunt, saying she'd likely surprise a few by attending. Mike Merrick told kennel managers his return would be early December.

The kennel knew to call his cell if his bird, cat, or dog showed behavior changes or illness, or issues about eating.

"Oh, this is simple and freeing, it's wonderful to leave!"

Mary and Mike caught the other smiling. Often. Their gazes met when spotting beautiful scenery. A heaven-sent break, Mary concluded. Mike's choice of music was perfect, too.

"I suppose we've decided it's agreeably okay to not wear masks when traveling together?" They both grinned.

In child-like fervor, joy soothed their insides, and semester angst shed per mile. The next weeks for him without university clamor. Mary caught herself looking forward to surprising her relatives. Two motel nights. A perfect span before flying home. Likely, it would be a small group due to the pandemic.

August the 2nd, by noon, the new leather smell blended well with the permeating sets of pheromones. When noticing her beige outfit exactly matching the upholstery, they laughed. "Why would a camping vehicle ever have light seat covers?"

"It matches the fur of my pets," Mike grinned, "next time they'll be with me. I already miss them." Light conversation planted odd impatience after 300 miles. She wanted to understand why he sought retrievals of unrelated studies.

He explained happily his collaboration with field scientists. Then, in laymen's terms, said, "Many days I assess and follow up on constant gatherings of latest data loads – for renewed test designing. It's contrasting and comparing builds!"

He went on describing topics of secondary research data and subsequent post phases. "Daily data arises everywhere. Always discussion on every single little aspect of data."

"See how important your job is, Mary?"

"Yes," she laughed. "The 'all I know is that I know nothing' is the humbling wisdom these days for me!"

For the next 110 miles they often switched topics. Early development of vans and campers. He talked about the 1910 Touring, a basic cart with folding seats, a Bertram launched it. Then minutes on development of puncture-proof tires.

Their lightness was pitched a curveball in the form of a billboard photo of a church, non-secularity prompting musing. Mary slowly drew cautious breath. Mike felt the shift in her energy, saw her facial expression light up and then dim.

"How many historical religions hadn't helped all humans equally? Don't get me started, but hey, only one gender's writings were published in most world religions' guidebooks!... you believe obedience and guilt are goals of nationalized religions?"

"Versions of golden rules?"

Her soft bluntness and his discipline's axioms bumped at the other. He defended his work. Cultural and social mores for centuries relied on 'humans willing to survive in sets of installments - for a prescribed greater purpose.'

"Coercing the furniture?"

"Most will profess belief because it began by suggestion or an obligation, or it was ordered by a power figure."

"Our planet sure is interesting."

"Yes, I read something last night that jolted my views on a lot. It was an astronomic essay. I learned elements are more abundant than others on different planets from other galaxies. Different proportions vary on each planet. Something a religious zealot on our planet ever addresses."

Mike switched jazz music to the 80's, then again to classical, back and forth, following his own mood or psychic toggle.

"Mary, there are millions of published works on faith and heavenly spiritual symbols. You know there's encyclopedic and there's non-fiction, there's news, and fiction. Science, humor, etc.

"As for scientific testing, religion remains hands-off, and most scientists see why. Tests aren't workable, can't be managed, are without consistency. Definitions differ regarding 'common good.' Remains categorized as unevidenced-based belief systems, not considered purely empirical.

However, most people believe in spirituality, even scientists do, it's said. If you can't adequately assess with results, you can't prove anything right or wrong. The test challenge stays. Remains in the heart and the belief. And hope.

He saw her rapid dull-penciled thoughts making way in her hand-made Squib Books. He imagined gifting her a moleskin or something better than her construction paper.

Mike wondered suddenly, given how she valued her privacy as much as he valued his, and how on this earth she'd met and bore a daughter with any father, and how long together, if at all.

She wasn't open to his thoughts, she already had hopped ahead, academic data subscription recently visited her dreams. "I will want the research librarian position, ah, when the job posts."

He hid his smile then chose not to respond.

She squibbed for the next two hours. He listened to baseball autobiographies. Redirecting her laptop, she located his list of data links. Easily, she found the studies on half of the list, then emailed them to him. Seldom did she put her work aside for more than five minutes to note scenery.

"Are you going to ask for links after settling in your camp?"

He darted a glance, chose not to provide a definite answer.

More miles north, a juice bottle resting by her ankle lost its cap, caused by a road bump, then the bottle rolled unnoticed, to under the seat. Their conversation drifted into deity depths, then branched into classic chimpanzees' territorial alertness studies.

"Survival and role definition was a famous one, keen on locating distant ripened fruit locations." Then he shared the adeptness of chimps in cognitive tests. Games involving working memory.

"Did humans score poorer? Really?"

"Go figure!" as he passed the exit highway sign.

He then backtracks, secures the chimp topic. Then again, he misses the exit sign. "Name famous studies regarding a chimp's short-term memory? Do they have self-awareness?"

They laugh like kids. Juice sloshes the carpet. Mary sets the laptop near her toes, searching for a sharp pen from her purse.

Again, she picks up on her Squib Book.

"Didn't sleep well last night," he apologizes.

Sunflower Grub Stop was next. While Mike pays for gas, Mary opens the glove compartment for a better pen. A photo lies in plain sight. In it, Mike's sitting with a very young blonde and pretty girl. He appears five years younger than now. It puzzles her why the photo is loose and alone like that. She flips it over. A phone number is written in his handwriting. Her name: Lucille.

The passed piloting exam and a copter test meant smooth flying and a flawless weekend ahead, but Janna won't stop talking to notice Jude's nervousness.

They argue for about two minutes into the blue on Sunday, the Junipers' wrangle volume reaches a milestone: "You *just didn't* listen!" Unnoticed, below is a canvas of sages, forest greens and slated blue acreage. His new money, she yells, is a candied band-aid! *Her* income supported it all! The city's mandate to close local parlors brought business clients these last few covid months.

Angry words harmonize with the copter's whirring old, whiny engine. Neither have inkling something could rise to alter things, big time. The beauty below and above remains unenjoyed.

They choose to yell at like mad baboons, high in the air.

Urgency knocks, though.

He lands the helicopter expertly. They'll each have to quickly run from the copter to find a bush. He'd had too much water before leaving, and she was sensing her monthly. On the way out of the copter, he grabs a cold can of beer.

Their offramp, at last! They have succeeded! Exciting! But the map's small print, Mike complains, doesn't name the roads!

His ink mark on the map indicates the exact location of the detour he'd planned on, but the van's GPS readout doesn't match the location or the street's name. Plus:

At the same time both realize the actual name on the road sign differs from GPS logic *and* the map. The sign is modern and shiny clean. Fresh new paint.

Mike slows, spots an entrance yards away. Tread imprints show vehicles had headed east, in the direction they wanted.

"Yes! here! The detour! The next 17 miles should save us way more than 30 minutes!"

Gravel digs in the tires. Mike decreases speed. Unkempt, dead branches extend over stretches. Rocks smooch tires. "To save time," he taps the map, though his tone has lost certainty. "Hooks onto two highways."

Mary tries to muffle her miff. Losing all subtlety, she yanks the map from his lap. "Where's the publication date? Oh. Four years old! I didn't give this to you! Where did you find it?"

"I found it in my own home atlas index…by myself! But if I'd had passwords, I'd been able to locate a more updated one?

You think? Maybe, Mary? Password rules should be altered."

"We're in the middle of bumpy dust-filled nowhere-villa and talking passwords? The county office would have mailed a map or guided you to the more recently approved ones!" She is surprised at the level of anger and her loudness.

"You are probably correct in that," he appeases.

"We both know how expensive subscription bundles are! Equivalent to a newly bought home mortgage!"

"University libraries weren't cheaply built. Nor vans."

"Oh, um, yes. Adding to that. Hey. Mike, I know this van is over-the-top pricey. Afford a subscription for yourself?"

"I love my van. Thank goodness for libraries and passwords -- or not." He points. The road ahead resembles a herded animal trail. "What the hay?"

"Should go back, no hurry to the reunion - really!"

"It'll join the other highway soon, it's supposed to!"

Mike's tension cuts every syllable. He grunts in low decibels. Her typed-in key words won't reap a thing, they only sludge in a lost connectivity. She slams the lid, angry, seeing now that her device is slippery, wet. It was soaking in the spilt juice.

The van wobbles. Stones and sharper wood chunks gnaw the tires. "The detour slice *was how many miles?*"

She stiffens. Now she squibs to '*brave it. Not. Then fake it though you'd be inauthentic.*' She snarls more, '*the semblance of positivity was meant to avoid harsh confrontation. I emphasize now and loudly here,*

Coping would require removing the scratching branches. His face reddens, she shouts, "You don't want scratches on this van! Stop this damned pearly pricy prima dona prize of yours!"

In panic he stops. Fifteen minutes of walking and breaking off clumps of twigs up to where the road begins to widen before they begin chuckling at themselves.

She tries the radio. It is dead. Then the player. The player works. She smiles when after three minutes the road becomes smooth, and the music soothes.

But the road is steep. Even more. First gear is needed.

Poor planning, bad foremen? A bulldozer stopped? Funding dried up, perhaps? The virus infected the workers?

The untrodden incline brought a thrust that jerks their heads. Upward turns give another 70 yards of chunky road riddling, side-dished with mud puddles, branches and large rocks.

He gropes, whispers "saving time" and is weakly assuring, nodding to condescend. Her teeth are clenched now. Bird release splats the shield. She is angry with herself for faking being okay.

Breathing slowly, deeply, and ….

"Wh-what the hey?" A big boom reverberates. All four tires elevate several inches then quickly slam down onto the gravel. Mike hits his head on the ceiling. Belts are ineffective. Both bounce and shout. Shocks absorb, then again, UP! Heads bam, then DOWN! Heads hit again! Airbags meet the seatbelts!

Her keyboard is now over-soaked. Ruined.

The sun too brightly punches stronger beams, blinding them. A tall blocking darkness gets bigger, then SMACK! Bark branches poke a harsh thrust to crack glass. He brakes. A second closer, its back side would have been crushed. Mike reverses. All tires uncontrollably slide then meet boulder sized rocks. The van turns over. Guttered, insect-infested potholes splash dance like dark laughter, a saddening stupidity.

Then over again. It's a pearly white tutu prop in its 10-hour old debut lutz. Just for an encore, a final slide begins when a second falling tree slams the van's back top.

Done. Both are in shock and are frozen, near unconscious. Mary's right-side is perpendicular, grounded. Jabbing door handles grind her right ribs. Her window features flat dirty soil and pebbles while the sky shows through his. Both now are out cold. Mike's head collapsed on her air bag's left side.

Dirt clouds rise.

No one anytime soon would adequately reason how four healthy trees fell on August 2nd, around 3:03 p.m.. Each de-rooted somehow, 27 yards away at the same second. Two fell one way and two fell completely oppositely.

Neither Mike nor Mary saw that set of trees fall, nor had glimpsed toward the sky to spot a sputtering copter's spherical drunken descent, foot-by-foot, to meet a welcoming cushion of pine branches which had landed seconds before. As though gifted somehow, it met its soft landing, its rotor blades pelleted.

When the pine hit the ground hard, their impact caused stones to pellet up high into the air.

Unsecured wine and gin bottles, pills, cosmetics, clothing, and other items spewed, hitting sides, beating up the screaming Junipers - into silence. Rolled bags bounced, remaining instrumental, saving both of their skulls.

But both hit to be conked out into silence.

Though no count was officially recorded, the exact number was 61 boomeranging rock pebbles holed the copter's twirling rotor blades. A seismograph recording station many miles away was working short; half of its crew, it was known, had been fighting the pandemic from home.

LUMINSTRATUM

Hues of blues, purples and grays play behind David Anthony and My Lady. They continue to communicate unshrouded by matter.

David Anthony: *That was something! I will send in a request to find out how those trees fell. Wow, so close. Cinematic.*

My Lady: *Sending them love of life and hope right now. Wondering what you like about being a sentinel when this happens. I won't be the finest, but I've made it to here.*

David Anthony: *We are all right, everything alters. Look! Glimpse PNW there, all for our understanding … we're speeding ahead to December! We'll switch and go back soon.*

My Lady: *The man is getting out of his van. The passenger seat has his wife.*

David Anthony: *I see something shiny. It's intentional.*

My Lady: *Look! The man found a tin-bound bundle!*

FAST FORWARD TO: DECEMBER 21, 2020, 2PM

Tires slow to stop, greeted by specks of snow. Feet inside a pair of $4,700 horsehide/calfskin boots step out of a tan rental van, to squish a mushing claylike soil clumping with pine needles.

Snow flecks hit boots as he pivots back to the rental van where a seated woman hands him a thick pair of leather gloves.

His intended area is more than twenty yards away where a vehicle rests, wrecked, on an adjacent, unpaved road.

"Washington is colder than I thought!" says the woman.

Yards from his boots, his eyes catch a glint. It's a square inch of silvery metal, peeking through a mound of muck. Parts of dirty-white soaked feathers have adhered to it. The man grasps and lifts. He wipes it with his pocket handkerchief.

Shine emits like lightning from this mass of flattened tin cans, pounded down, wire-bound, and now encasing a 225 cubic inch mass. It's protecting something. More soaked white feather parts are caught within the wire's twists.

He turns his head toward the van, "Call Gina!"

Tomorrow, Gina will skip having the boots cleaned, she'll have already sent replacement pairs delivered to their lodge.

Snow keeps increasing steadily in speed and volume.

His foot kicks the mass to scoot it from the mushy area, the tin wrapping is lightweight, sliding farther than predicted.

His humming is heard through his hoodie, mask and goggles. It's an uplifting, soft tune which now is dancing the snap of tin snipping. His partner, warmed by a blue shawl gives a smile, "this needs recording." Even with her frail, shivering arms, she finds the sound and video button.

"What song are you humming?"

It is new to him, he explains. Even he hasn't ever heard it.

"It was nice to hear!"

He sits back into the cab behind the wheel, sets the block on his lap. "Humming diverts discomfort. Like when freezing."

More shinier slivers of tin layers beckon removal. He peels them as his teeth rattle. Breathing pure white clouds even while inside the vehicle. Snowpacks are covering the shield.

"I don't want to see my face or hear me in social media!"

"That would be a first!"

Minutes later, after peeling and bending back another tin layer, both receive a cautionary flash of yellow pad with blue lines. Needed now is ultra careful peeling, he didn't want to rip.

"Let's ditch here and get by the fireplace at the lodge, read the yellow pad after dinner! GPS better work, it's too blinding."

"And I'm an iceberg!"

An hour later, a fireplace throws warmth. It's beside a window showing solid white outside. His hands are now ungloved. She asks lodge helpers to bring hot chocolate and watches her husband remove the first yellow, blue-lined tablet. The ink is blue. Subsequently tucked are more tablets. All is in either red, green, or black ink; each handwriting is unique.

"When the snow stops, we'll go right back to check out the wreck!" The help at once checks the weather and announces what emails are now there for them to read and respond to.

The woman begins reading two intro handwritten pages. They are both enthralled immediately by the content, the meaning of the words. The plan now is for extremely late reading. First, put piano music on.

Back to the Wrecked Van Camp (WVR)

August 2, 2020

Four wreck victims groggily awakened although stunned, emotionally numb, and in searing pain. Foggy minds try to understand how and what brought them to this, they drift back into a mindless episodic trauma of choppy, distorted dreams.

Attaining levels of clarity isn't yet a goal. It is dusking.

The van's engine still purrs. An 80's song bumps from a damaged player. Words intended to convey someone's love, *She depends on it, so much'* crookedly fail to soothe, since smashed speakers, now out of sync, let out words '*sh - deep sh*t on smush.*'

Lost tempo.

Mike snores. Mary whimpers.

Birds circle then land on cracked windows before switching direction to fly off. They look straight through, behind the glass, seemingly to notice humans in the car. Mary and Mike are feeling mean confusion. Their limbs, backs, necks, wrists, faces, and torsos pierces. They're bloody. They cannot face the other, so both let out a groan to signal each has life inside.

The Juniper's don't yet note a thing to measure. The severity of their injuries will soon cast them brutally into a new unwelcoming reality of painful entwinement. The cabin is tiny.

No one in either wreck is ready to even consider what to do tomorrow or predict with accurately any likelihood of a handicapped life. Catastrophe has muted everything.

Minutes pass quickly. Both Junipers are slow to note the packed vs. loosened items and are cringing while fumbling. Janna digs carefully into pockets for meds. In the dimming light she locates pain pills from recent cosmetic surgeries. Meeting trouble she opens its lid and then swears when checking Jude out. She sees Jude's expired pain relievers left over from dental surgery. Struggling to scoop, she retrieves more than needed. They spill on the copter's ceiling now serving as their floor.

Back in the van, Mike sleepily figures he must connect to 911. Both hips and index fingers only feel pain, so numbness signals him to slow. After rubbing his hand on his thighs, he tries twice to dial punch 911. No connectivity. He'll try later.

He'd planned to pick up an ordered cell tower booster from an outlet near his sabbatical camp. He regrets the choices made.

No surveillance, no rescue arrivals.

Mary is still, yet she is breathing.

Jude feels Janna's hand placing a new pill in his. Droopily, he glimpses out the cracked window. He sees the holes in the rotor blades. Refurbish the blades! Newest art! After fifteen minutes, with doped glee, he concludes that rocks did this. Or someone with a gun? If there was a gun, there'd be trouble.

Now he feels so good. He whispers his chuckle to not hurt rib muscles, then pops another half pill, and chases it with wine.

Yes, inside those blade holes, cement in rhinestones! Sparkling pellet holes! What a topic of conversation to sell it with!

He'd pitch by saying, "Oh, this!" he'd point to his art piece, "I survived a crash because leafy pines saved my butt. Yes, this wind-chimed dangler is rotor blades!" He laughs. It would be just another brilliant pandemic product. Add that to his mountain of created junk beauty, and no thanks to covid closed art fairs.

The meds work for injury pain but punctuate his hysteria. He recalls that farmers' markets were open during the pandemic, selling essentials. It would have been a better destinated choice.

He'd been careful with his stimulus money. Thank goodness his dad had been a saver. The inheritance check would be in his hands when they got home. He feels happy again, but no Avatar meet-up will occur now. For them.

Something's cracked near his jaw. He rummages through Janna's purse for her compact mirror. His free hand bumps her forearm. She howls. Her facial skin is bruised. He visualizes an art canvass, and an oil paint color identical to those bruise colors. "Ouchy Burgandy!" he speaks loud enough for Janna's eye to open half-way. "Have another?" he places a tablet on her tongue.

He succumbs to dream, 'Purplyepiderm' - the best title of the painting when he gets around to it.

Janna dreams she's speeding loosely through the sky; her collar is clamped by a beak. It's a black and white bird with an avatar head resembling a handheld hairdryer, and it pecks a window then pulls out pink sponge hair-roller shaped worms.

Yards away, Mike dreams, too. In it he repairs the van's windshield cracks, shredding printed abstract pages. He shapes them into pea-sized baseballs and bats by first moistening them with bottle spilled juice. He then fills the van's window cracks.

He awakens to see drooped, limping shards.

Mary's reverie has her in the nursing department gazing at shelved library atlases and world religion books. She rests on a cot, cataloguing map books. The location, though, is inside the library lab. Plastic dummies move robotically, dressed like nurses attending dummy patients. Two have Mary's cousins' faces, ones likely to be attending the reunion. They ooh over bloody cuts but can't wrap perfectly, so Mary snatches the maps from them.

The real time, not-a-dream sprained arm jerks in sync with

the reverie's snatching one. Piercing wakeful pain prompts her to whine loudly to awaken Mike. He then jumps to hurt himself, too, and then bangs his head on the steering wheel. Both sit, cringing in silence while gazing at the sunset through several limping, dusty dangling windshield shards. She looks sideways at him and wants to smile, change all this, make it all a slapstick joke.

One shard is now square on Mike's lap. He inhales too quickly, smarts, then carefully picks it up to poke the airbag reset button. Mary thinks his purple forehead gives his humiliated ape-like appearance more cinematic character with all that has happened. and can't stop thinking about the stupid sapiens in this wrecked van. The whisper how crazy bad this all is.

Grappling hope, Mike visualizes small vehicles venturing this far in, if a driver can brave it. Or be as stupid as he had been?

The wrecked van is unmissably dead center on the path.

Coyote pups with their mom circle a colony of bunnies. Seven very large white birds glide over. Do birds qualify the scene below them? All spectacles? Mike smiles suddenly, noticing how quickly the bunnies dart underneath the coyotes, circling to cause clumsy confusion before finding cover.

"Good luck," they both whisper.

Fifteen yards up, a bald eagle is branched, watching it all as the sun's rays refract light from the mangled metal. Pink and orange rays are beautiful, almost psychedelic.

In hours the fully waxed moon will be the only light. Mike must figure how to maneuver out of the wreck, to build a fire.

He will need to apologize to Mary. She'd missed her timeline. Good intentions hadn't succeeded. For now, he remains shamefully quiet with worry. And his heart won't stop aching.

Emergency response measures haven't arrived. All four, in separated consciousness levels realize this hard reality. Only isolation. Help will come, believe it. Stomachs growl with hunger.

Jude envisions his ex-wife soon will send their seven-year-old son to ask for money if they aren't rescued in a few days. A "missing" status could officially get filed.

Both Junipers want wine, are wincing, and wondering how many unbroken booze bottles there might still be.

Adding regret to aches, Mary reviews. She'd only RSVP'd one forgetful aunt named Madeline about reunion attendance and without non-disclosed full commitment. Colleagues and daughter or neighbors would not picture anyone with her.

Regretful, she figures rescue could be soon.

Mike murmurs he's worried over the welfare of his animals.

Arms can't reach through the van's mess, its floor a wall. Fallen items block access to utilities. How much food? A solar panel, if not crushed, means food could last. He'd overpacked water bottles. A brook should be somewhere.

Better, a Samaritan motorcyclist, via that awful detour holding a surplus of needs in his backpack -- and connectivity. There's relief, people are good. Mike sends this to the universe.

He decides to use his skull to push his driver's side door, the side window now a skylight. He grunts as toes meet squish.

It's totally covered in mud, dust, pine parts and twigs. After three scoop-outs, the pearly white says a sad, wounded shameful puncture toned hello. He muffles his gasp, he shouldn't cry.

His chest and throat swell. He swallows. Feathers tickle his nose. He needs to knock out a sneeze. Staring directly at a bright silver sliver left of the sun can speed up the inevitable.

Do it loud, and long and a lot. Allow me to mask it.

He releases an avalanche of sobs alongside the sneezes.

Mary can hear it all anyway. Her cut, bloodied lips quiver, her throat swells. "Need a tissue?" she whispers, not to be heard.

Mike wipes his nose and resumes the task of making this time bearable. His eyes search for something stint-like to set his right leg. A splintered baseball bat-colored branch pokes for his attention from the rear cracked window. His early year toddler's memory resurfaces horror seeing his new tricycle rolling off a cliff. The van is done. He sobs, forgets to muffle.

Still inside the car, Mary fails without pain to reach the armrest of the high sky-facing door. His bumping around outside bass line the groove of foul words she hadn't heard him yet use.

She whispers she agrees 100%.

Can she just connect anywhere? Pads, phones, and laptops – not even a pillow. She flinches then checks her cuts; it's time to rise to the task of exiting out of the van.

Outside he blares "the detour road is a thoroughfare to hell, and it wasn't what the map showed!"

Neither knew Mike had missed the right one - his planned slice for a detour. Yet, the poor one they ended up on moments ago was being blockade. Newly painted signs just seconds ago were cemented in the rocky dirt.

And three motorcycles had been directed to stay out.

Scheduled for Monday, tomorrow, August 3rd, heavy chains would close all off. A legal sale was signed, the small print reveals.

DON'T ENTER. Coded lines warn of fines if ignored.

The intended detour road was 20 yards from the dooming path. It would have quickly, smoothly, successfully delivered Mary to hook up on the road to her reunion site. Unfortunately, a year before, a temporary wall was installed to block entry and view. Current maps hadn't reached the wider communities. Navigation registered incorrectly with new road signs and GPS's.

Within seven months construction would begin.

Mush greets her landing feet. She slips and slides like a toddler, then splashes bottom first into a buggy pond. Disruption again! Mike stops his progress of building a fire. "Setting up a stove will wait.," He walks limping badly to her, offering a shaky hand, seconds don't pass without one of them sliding and saving.

Each heard the scurrying squirrels in the shrubbery.

She'll receive his offer to use his pillow.

"Those blankets stay for now!" He points to the van's rack, "My knife breaks rope tomorrow. Tonight's warm."

Settling uncomfortably on a lawn chair, she wants to write a list of mounting to-dos. Attempts to fetch a pencil bring only pain but it doesn't matter, she is so tired and hurting. It doesn't matter that she has no idea where her Squib book is.

First, she wants to ask him something.

That photo of a young girl sitting with Mike. How does she inquire using healthy gracefulness? *It isn't to be named healthy or not healthy right now.* It is not an urgent matter. Never mind, not now.

"Is this a flipping nightmare?" she yells instead, glaring. He winces. "Don't answer!" she continues, "Solitude! Quiet up, everyone for a while!" Her snarl surprises and stiffens Mike.

If this crippled, dwindling energy could simply rise to allow her to dig to find her Squib book, maybe pain would divert. And hey, think positive! Help could come sooner than they thought!

In the dimness she glances at her mirror. Bloody cheeks, blackened eyes. She gasps repeatedly; it is a shock to see. After five minutes checking every inch of her body, slowly, and hurting while doing so, she quietly admits it.

She hadn't wanted to renew with cousins; she remembers scenarios. Avoidance. Meddling ones intrusively pried out 'secrets' to just pass around. Nosiness. Simple curiosity were not deep concerns. That was her family. Most disliked each other.

Mary quietly seethed, remembering power struggles. Did any attain self-aware expansiveness or intellectual growth? That same dynamic occurred during Meghan's birth. She'd analyzed not sharing her values with Dave's. Maybe all of them, herself included, were wrapped up in themselves - perhaps borderline narcissists? That rogue word again!

And the epiphany of the hour: she realized the reunion should have NEVER been mentioned with Mike. Never!

Everything exponentiated. Here she is. Likely, at this minute, her relatives are fighting over pandemics and politics.

Farther away from the bugs, Mike wrestles, still in crucial pain. He tries not to share it. He slowly sets the sleeping bag by the campfire, adds branches while clenching, enduring.

She is quieting her pained wails after each habitual reflex.

"Mary" is the only sound he can now respond with, out of his heavy heart, deep in his chest, amplifying his sad voice. He coaches himself inwardly to find humor she might like, he'd like, maybe they'd like. Both could smile to help through a moment. Hocus pocus for the happiness.

"Worthless key words! This is ruined!" He watches Mary's new habit of failing at her keyboard; showing craze, she slams it shut with another smart. "I needed to retrieve 'regional bugs!'"

His cue for braving it has widely arrived, given him light.

Attempt the 'dim dry dig' humor on her. She is harmless as a disabled. Can't throw something or hit him.

"So," he risks, "how 'bout querying 'Camping Blogs'… Nah. What about 'Setting Boundaries in Brokenness,' No, too dark. 'Bruised, Bugged and Busted' Oh, bad one. Maybe better, the 'National Organization of Lid Slamming Librarian Forums?'"

He's a ham, she thinks, and can't stop her smile.

"Maybe, 'Reunion Bug Cousin Casserole Contests!'"

"Well, why don't we both write two gargantuan SOS's by scooting our bums on the dirt to form those letters? In that way you won't jerk your arms. You'd only get dirty pants."

"Crusty roasted bug recipes on marshmallows with chocolate colored insect juice."

"No Mores."

Pained groaning shorts out two potential chuckles, perhaps creating a funny duet. Their volume doesn't scare the birds which are free to fly away, though. Instead, they choose to stay in a new, questionable vibration right now, at this site.

Fast Forward, Again, December 21, 2020–

MAN WITH THE BOOTS BY THE FIREPLACE

Well-manicured male's hands gently turn the 5"x7" yellow, blue-lined pages. Outside, the mad wind whips, stronger than yesterday's blizzard. Forecast is that the sun will peep in two or three days. An aproned lady softly enters then makes sure they're comfortable beside the fire --- and equipped.

"Settle in, here's chocolate."

They plan to read and reread every single page.

Each page holds succinct writing. So far, all appear composed neatly. He assesses the writer as a highly learned, comprehensive builder, a man reflecting authentically, who has realized the terms of his situation. He won't settle with defined fate and believes this experience could be valuable - to someone.

And that the man named Michael Merrick is brave.

Yesterday's short visit showed no sign of human activity. He'd get a better scoop later, with more visibility. Loosened items were scattered, collecting snow and cones. A pup tent had been leaning and had stood wobbling throughout strong winds.

The pages' dating revealed a longer time span most humans could survive without food. He'd noticed yesterday multiple charred trees near the tin-bound bundle. Fire in September? Nothing yet had suggested life or human movement.

Already he and his wife have planned who they'll call in the next hours regarding investigating whatever Merrick was about.

Tin wired block found December 21, 2020.

Introductory note to whoever finds the following 52 yellow pages:

My name is Dr. Professor Michael Merrick, writing this quick introductory page, needing to explain quick what it is and why before I enclose this into a flattened tin can covering. The following will show what I experienced and wrote daily. What brought me to be stranded here was an unfortunate, devastating accident on August 2, 2020, when tall, healthy pine trees fell and my new van was wrecked (& practically crippled us). 'WVC' is 'wrecked van camp'. Librarian Mary Hawkings was my van passenger.

*Someone could check August 2nd 2020 seismograph records in this area? The following described phenomenal accounts will interest experts of several disciplines. My records will require highly learned deciphering, decrypting, decoding. I will here add prayers, at times, too. I became a constantly praying person while here.

Again, my intro "preface" is being written as quickly as the <u>wildfire is spreading a few miles away.</u> Sound recordings are hopefully stored in my alternate cell phone, inside the wrecked white van's (WV stands for wrecked Van) glove compartment.

Most recorded incidents occurred ¾ of a football field from where you likely located this bundle – at the base of the nearest large hill and a cave.

I've been charging cell phones daily, thanks to

64

solar energy. No connectivity elsewhere.

The western sky is now very orange, brown with smoke; flames are quickly growing.

Also, quickly, I must add that I might have utilized agent-based modeling methods (internet availing) - simulated entirely in fictional form. NO juice arrived.

Dr. Michael Merrick, Professor and Researcher

Back to AUG 2, 2020. 9:00 p.m.

Mike cannot sleep, so he decides to creep around carefully to inspect the surroundings. Mary's resting body is calm, now, on pebbly ground, wrapped in a jacket.

With a whisper he says goodnight to her, taping a note to '*Bang and alert me. Don't hurt your arms!*' on the side of a metal bowl. Taped on it is a silver spoon he'd already set beside her. Pained arms tomorrow shall dig into the Wrecked Van's (WV) shrew for whistles to blow in case wild things venture too close to the make-shift camp.

Moon beams cast blue batik patterns and tickle crevassed slopy grounds. He paces steps carefully. His backpack slightly rocks. Oatmeal bars and bottled water are heavy enough to prohibit deep breaths which hurt his rib muscles. More slowly, he exhales and stays dizzy due to the minimally required amount of oxygen. He sits down.

Magnificently, the starlit sky sooths him with twinkling clusters and mesmerizes him. He pivots to face Mary; his heart wishes to say, look up at this!' or 'goodnight!' Instead, he clears his throat loudly. She doesn't stir. He walks to her pillow to softly drop bars and bottled water beside her bruised, pretty face.

He leaves her. She sleeps.

Dust tickles his nose. Don't sneeze, he orders, savor hefty pine scents. The sneeze wins, anyway, and as he feared, again, his rib muscles pierced. He yelps. He checks. She didn't awaken.

Tree limbs suddenly rustle, letting loose a gliding bald eagle, deciding to fly upward. Too soon it's silhouetted by the largest, most beautiful he's ever seen a full moon to be. He feels love.

Suddenly an odd yet beautiful oval-shaped bluish puddle draws him in, closer. He decides it is not water. It's an intermittent glow, not reflecting anything. Is it nano bionic, a light-emitting plant? A whitish stack of particles? In two walking minutes he'll touch it. Maybe.

It eerily draws him in, his heart starts to race. Ethereal.

Zinc sulfide? Strontium aluminate - the stuff in toy wands giving off that jolly phosphorescent glow-in-the-dark allure, that's it. Toys. Boy's bedroom walls! He smiles. Baseball mitts, pitchers, batters; a collective finale, a nightie-night seductive show.

Nearer, he sees pulsating lights peeking through.

He gulps. A white bird-feather pile? Wings so large, stacked high! Parts of broken branches obscure glow in places. Not a toy. His wobbly light finds intricate, woven patterns throughout the feathers. Were these collapsed wings or broken ones? A flock of egrets? They don't appear damaged. Poor birds, dead?

His two African Greys' image appear, as do dozens of past encounters with white doves. Large as an Albatross? Not near enough to the ocean. White pelicans? No, too inland.

He remembers tasting cornflakes, at age seven inside the

kitchen nook, reading cereal box comics, noting wallpaper's grey heron art, and snowy owls, ones his mother loved to collect.

Visualizing dead birds brings shudders. Death in real time dizzies his innards, his hands, which shake his flashlight grip. His mouth waters to advance his chuck. But he pictures Mickey Mantle hitting the ball out of the park. Or Joe Dimaggio. Imagination proves reliable, serving him often as an antidote. Ralphing fails. Why Mickey's? He hasn't probed. It just works.

Like magic, the silver-fringed detailed wing pattern is a fine, platinum sheen and he feels a warmth massaging his back.

His fear lessens. A torn-off bird's leg is lit by his flashlight, then a detached bird's head. He jolts. Feathers don't match one another. Had birds, if they were birds, been blasted down?

Fresh release lumps haven't dried. Saliva's forming a puddle in his mouth. Babe Ruth time or Mickey again? Closing his eyes and grappling blindly with the loose broken branches and soil, he covers to protect the more beautiful feather parts.

Minutes later he has positioned pebbles into shapes on the ground as a psychology symbol, and a social symbol. It is to find it later if necessary.

Again, he adjusts to the sight of scared phosphorous light bits looking at him - coyote eyes blinking. It is dusty and earnest.

A familiar scene? Mike's mind asks it. Back again, for more bird meal maybe? Are you the killer? Had your band feasted here? Was there a fight to live, or were these wings of aviary carcasses? Predictably, the coyote darts away.

Yards away, Janna's body is contorted because the copter's floor is half the width of her regular bed. Euphoric pills and moonlight through broken glass windows give her a web pattern to marvel upon Jude's face. She giggles, ignoring her battered arms. Her legs won't move. Bones broken? Everything hurt an hour ago, and she smiles now. Will she assess tomorrow when trying to walk?

In a pilled state, she dreams of her sister, Sheryl, who had once met a man at an online singles' site, then swooped fast into an elopement. Sheryl says, "Social life's a game. Most regret missteps, others don't care, some become accountable. But Baby Janna, dear one, do lose the avatar stuff. Be real and true."

She awakens to Jude's stirring and sees a bulge in his jean pocket. An entire pill canister? Would either need all that for only three days? Hooked? She wants one, he gives two. A messy reality. Chase it with booze.

Minutes later, Jude's snoring stopped.

August 3rd in Boston, 1:00 a.m.

Being next door to the best research library was one out of ten smart moves all week so far; Marchers, five weeks ago, agreed for a November 2020 meeting. In a throb and a breath Rhetta landed in New York days after receiving their thumbs up. She rented a 340 square foot room surrounded by multiple city and national socioeconomic cultures! But she was shifting, fading, losing something and she was very worried suddenly.

She counted the plusses: Community associative librarians with great open-ended research questions would be of great help.

But so far, daily moods have ranged, though, from fearlessness to paranoia with portions of low confidence. Stability could be restored in her gut if she suddenly decided to return to the community center job. Aging without question in a pigeonholed career was a minimally secure journey compared to here, suddenly knowing one wrong move could kill hope during this 'here and now' wonderment.

Digging deeper, it didn't feel right. Being alone and lost was not new to her, but having recently through a letter and phone call promised a mogul some great work was scarier than she'd previously had acknowledged. She knew not the right ropes or what to do. The idea of meeting and having something great for him to consider was false; she had absolutely nothing right now. She had acted on ignorant hopeful impulse.

Obligated to find a way to give back? Such a weakened cliché: to give back.' No, obligated to figure out why my current life is unfulfilling. Today and always, there was/is something not perfectly hitting the mark. Fancy desires compete now with the pull to find the truth. A constant study. She sneered. Spoiled damned humans of today. Call it the 'human condition' or 'the half empty' cup. Selling answers in books when attaching a trendier label to define it with a new cure.

She shook her head, put it in her hands. Am I a fraud? The ill-equipped but passionate struggler was more grateful than she. *And, no, I don't need a different savior even though I've messed up big time, several times, Is wanting to make a difference without knowing exactly what for translate I've poor mental health? Wanna be famous. All this is* seeded by advertisement, greed to persuade the consumers. All from the top down. Always.

What to focus on first? Unless zeroing soon and deeply in on research, she'd have nothing to show in November. Before today, she'd felt big with ideas and solutions. Now having committed to meeting Marcher, her block meant starting to question herself in every aspect.

Complete it. Commit. Plan to have your best work ever done for Marcher by November. He and his wife are progressive.

They care about the future of people, the country, the world. Rhetta drew in her guides. Thoughts fueled. She looked at the desk showing the Marchers' Business Journal articles besides her own certificates and degrees. Stationed them to self-motivate. Her plane itinerary was on the bulletin board, posted also. November was soon.

She'd asked in the letter to allow her to show them her research. Even then she hadn't a solid idea outlined for the Santa Barbara meeting at his mansion, one of many. Okay, Get Set!

She had three months to complete.

Honestly, it is okay, she soothed herself. Okay to form an important niche for herself for the resst of her life. Right? Clear the path. Be grateful, not married for security, she reminded herself, had steered from bonding with Mr. Wrong for her.

Thank Kelli for this. Amen.

A serious, good-looking mature girl, not ready for owning the 'woman' stature, playfully blew herself a kiss from the full-length mirror. Placing her mat on the wooden floor, she got on her knees and prayed while tearing off her clothes. *Be bare. Be real. Don't carry inside yourself your own lies.* After an hour of connecting to her childhood image of her deity, she worked yoga exercises to eclectic music for two hours. Ending with a deeply honest meditative candlelit prayer, her words formulated honest clarity.

Advance. She vowed that in the next weeks; three different social challenges would formulate for her. Marchers would likely support the best – if it benefited many large groups – and themselves and their cronies, too, just like every other billionaire.

Remember this time. Savor it, she told herself as she studied again the room's old wooden floors, poster bed, desk, kitchenette, and bath. The window seat offered space to people-watch. Her desk would remain orderly and her calendar would be checked hourly. She would be emailing confirmations weekly to the Marcher's meeting coordinators.

Her cell rang. Friends. She shortened them, she must delve. Today, she explained, "Can't be my chat day!" It's a renewable energy grid report and a health care affordability one. No time for partying tomorrow, either! "I am focusing on greenhouses, and solar panel roofs. Chunnels for chickens, you name it, it's on my list. Health care disparities? Migrants? Low-cost education? Studying today and tomorrow and the next on influentials. Philanthropic moguls. Follow it, smell the money."

Hill Base, August 2nd, Midnight

This first night in PNW brought heavy self-recrimination. Walking too slowly on an animal trodden path Mike felt heavy sleepiness above the gnawing pain. *This is what being ripped up feels like.* The day's flaws. He, the driver, only he, Professor Dr. Merrick, Mikey, who'd ignored obvious newly installed street signs – and signs incongruent with out-of-date maps and the GPS. He, the study builder. He felt the blame. He accepted it.

Over confidence? Is this happening to his profession? A player standing in center field in a half-built stadium, a bottom inning. His team was losing. Sigh. He inhales the aromatic pines.

As over-flying birds cut through the moonbeams, magically, his pain and doubt lessen. He'd make it up to Mary.

Now he must rest his aching head. Godawful in every cell of his body. *Go straight, right now to that slope near that hill.* Speed up a tad. Locate a soft, grassy knoll.

His steps slow down so not to exasperate ligaments. The moon and flashlight pick a drey of weakened squirrels. Are they too weary to hide new birth? *Don't let them distract you, don't pause, find your spot, just rest your aching head on the backpack for your pillow.*

Only five yards away, Mike completely misses the Juniper's copter. Misses it even with its upright dusty skids throwing back moonlight through many cradling branches. An upended nose.

An owl succeeds in gaining notice, though. It blinks. Mike says hello, then wonders again why owls are considered so wise. One across from it is white. White owls see the best over other owls. He remembers this from a zoology course.

He'll stare upward when finally reclining on the grassy mound. Just a few yards away! *Stars, please continue with your magic.* He prescribes a supine position, a backpack for the neck.

Try to just rest, stop hurting.

Trying to reach REMs, he summons images of stadiums, then imagines a faint cheering out of the fans. Less than a minute passes, he feels drifting. His body slowly slumps.

It that Music? Soft, it kisses ears on his head, so incredibly beautiful. It's faint. Does he hear this beautiful jewel of exquisiteness? Not linking a known instrument, but whatever, it's caressing, filling his body, his limb pain has disappeared.

Then a ringing, a tinkling? Maybe chimelike?

Not his summoned baseball park accolade, he sleeps, deeply - or is this a wakeful dream? Questioning his precise state places him in bewilderment.

His snoring wakes him. He hadn't wanted to sleep long. That ringing instrument a while ago, was it still sounding? No. Quiet. Had he dreamt of such soothing beauty? It existed, or not?

A fainter chime then starts up, affirming a waking reality.

He hears from parts deeper into the hill, from where ringing vibrations emanate. A cave. He's apprehensive, insecure.

A humming, vocal lullaby joins in. Voices unlike anything he's heard, as though in syllable yet foreign form, from another planet light up with emotional dazzlement. Nothing is understood. New energy weaves its uniqueness in pitch and tone. Cadence softly rocks and fills his body again with gladness. Light, pure light. Pure joy. Hope. Enormous Love.

He translates all as a powerful message, but wisely questions intention if fatefully directed to him. He feels drugged.

He'd only taken a few aspirins.

Humans rarely realize the full degree to which their five senses fail them. None can fully capture the capacity of frequency and vibration, force of chemo sensation or the force and clarity needed for sight. He's been aware of that. Sensory systems are relatively diminutive when compared to all the kingdom. Senses function however they can message the brain. Human brains are junked up, spoiled and unwilling to be utilized maximally.

Would hearing aids capture more? His last hearing exam passed. Identifying the instrument's material or shape for creating the sounds? Not quite metal, or string, no....

Being young and clueless, memories emerge with high school chemistry questions. Mendelevium categorizes transitional, metallic elements, of unfound elements which are likely to remain unnoted - and therefore uncategorized. Is the collection for the elementary table – or more correctly put, the periodic table – in infancy? A human's tool to categorize everything their universe throws at them?

Not brass, nor percussion. Grasping at straws, he is cognizant of, but he was open to continuing exploring and suddenly Mike remembers Dave.

It took centuries to form and agree on rules – but he understood it a work-in-progress - According to an adjunct faculty astronomy professor Dave, who had a double major in chemistry, and was scholar of outer space's compositional nature.

"Everything is ongoing with metals out there, so much in the works. So many complexities, compositions!" Dave had said.

That discussion didn't continue. He'd heard Dave was either let go or didn't make contract faculty or had expired.

Now Mike recalls the transitional metals shooting out from stars conversations - or lectures that had Mike's eyes glaze over.

Instead of studying chemistry very deeply in high school, Mike remembers how he instead chose to construct a fun Social Psychologist's "element" table having types of people: Some were catalysts. Careless ones, some very sensitive, some worth a lot in group positive interaction, others that loved bonding, etc.

His question tonight was not answered. His asking was real, it was current. How could glowing wings and sounds be able to temporarily soothe his back and legs? And mystify? And bring faith?

And then -

Floored! Dang! He woke. He'd slept *again!* Without remembering, drifting. Was this now twice? Mike feared losing awareness, self-control, his mind.

He grabbed a small pad and pencil.

'This was as if anesthetized, a black curtain drawn, and it not fading out, it was more like conking out.' He wrote each thought down, then continued detailing, capturing with remembrances, forcing his

pencil hard on the pad. Descriptions of it even being death.

August 3rd, Dawn

But again, he awakes as the morning's hot sun hits his face! Was he just writing, lit by the moon and a tiny flashlight? On a small pocket pad? Could he have dreamt of holding a pencil? Dreamt of writing on his pad? Dreamt of sounds, wings, the owl? Was the crash a dream? Maybe this was part of what dying is like.

Behold, his pencil is present! It's near his hand, still! What a relief! Thinking it not quite a full relief because the crash was real, he frantically scurries to locate the pad – wherever it might be – there! Right beside his foot! He turns the pad over to check.

Thank all Gods! All thoughts, all he wrote was all there! That part is not a dream. Joy streams all through his body. He sighs, smiling, realizing he'd written a lot, some near illegibility.

He'll never forget the music, whatever it is. Ever. This is overlapping a waking reality, and he admits how scary this has become, yet very much liking how dreams were out of this world.

No humming, no chimes, no bells, nothing. It's quiet but wrong to stay longer, Mary had been alone for way too long. He'll start to limp back but first he will check the wing pile, then search for a brook. He panics. He thinks they might run out of water.

Something wants and waits for him to see. He doesn't yet know, he tells himself. But he knows.

Sun refracts light peeking through tree branches. A metallic mass blares, camouflaging leaves, cock-eyed, dented. Cracked, dusty windows beg for a look inside. A pitiful upside-down kit, a four-seater suffered when parking? Studying the bullet-holed blades, had someone used a gun? Did this occur recently?

Anything, any person inside?

Likely, the copter met the earth yesterday, he concludes. It had also bounced to park atop pine pile limbs. Fresh ones, those pine trees. Four trees fell yesterday, then. Any authorities? Impact recorded? Government workers anywhere? Scarce during these recent erratic pandemic months...

Were there survivors of the crash?

Closing-in slower than ever with new down step pain, Mike is six feet away. He gulps. Any death inside? Ones could be needing help, but his best scenario would be there's absolutely nobody. His stomach can't. Necrophobia here.

Was it possible last night's sounds were of ones who'd arrived inside this copter? Copter musicians hiding in the cave?

Unprotected by 'the' university's ivory tower, without support staff, he decides to turn away, aware he is sidestepping. Knocking at his conscience is importance of confirming.

But not now.

If dead people are in there, he'll feel sick. He'd prefer to return to Mary, likely she's wondering. He heads toward the WVC. Too quickly his legs make him groan loudly. He must stop.

At a family funeral once, his mom said, "Corpses won't bite, Honey. Be respectful at least. A customary gesture from the living." His mom's voice often kidded while consoling.

Through that filthy window, he will try a look. His flashlight and wooden stick drop, then sweat near his belt buckle trickles to tickle his navel. Pained, he stretches to peek. The sun's glare blocks. *Focus*, he orders, then spies a red pooling, half dried.

Four stiffened legs appear to have wrestled.

He cannot see the faces.

Their bodies suggest attempts were made to snuggle. Two different colors of flesh show bloody gashes. He freezes with phobia. Baseball hero scenario mantras aren't recallable; all is too far gone. Nothing shows up to help him work with all this.

He looks away, diverts. The nausea is winning.

Eight appendages stiff? Mike says to himself, "breathe" aloud, his heart thumps in his neck seeing a pair of blue and orange oxfords and two bare dark-skinned feet, ankle-braceleted and tattooed. Disheveled curly dark hair is half covered by sleeping bags. He gently tries rocking the kit, using his unbruised knee, then turns to throw weight with his buttocks. He whimpers.

He yells, "Hello, hello!"

Nothing.

Shaking exaggeratedly, his knees won't hold up, he crumbles to descend, his backpack receives his head instead of the rocks. He yells as every blunted bruising soreness triggers. He folds over. He heaves. Dry wretches produce nothing.

His mouth still waters.

Amass guidance. Rescue teams will remove these bodies. Hopefully soon! And five steps away, heading toward the WVC, his mom's voice again. Bend carefully, fetch a rock. Throw it, hit the copter. Alarm everything alive. Do it. He does. His muscles forbid him to throw it stronger; it whimpers a ping.

Loudly, "Hello! Sorry! I'd call 911 but only with cell towers! There aren't any! I'll return, and until then rest in peace!"

"So pitiful," to no one in particular. "Please don't let ever a student or woman witness me at this!" then again wretches.

He heads toward the wing pile.

A doe and two shaky legged fawns sniff the wing pile. Mike wipes acidy moisture from his mouth. "Wild world for very dear deers." An owl flaps its heavy wings, then perches on the highest layer of the feather pile. Likely he's the same as last night's owl. Its glare penetrates Mike's. Owls owned environments.

Mike muses, he wants to describe this to Mary.

New York, Lunchtime

Rhetta dreams of a philanthropic circus tonight, there's loud music. A community theater stages a younger Rudy, mouthing a song, showing huge teeth, protruding lips, both hiding behind a huge mustache. He's off-key.

There she is with people celebrating 'Benevolence Night' and Rudy dances with symbolic 'benevolence figures,' wearing banners. Every single sign has: 'More Toward ALL Humanity's Future.' Deciphering each dancer's true form is difficult. Each with causes claiming to perpetuate happiness for all. She holds a box named 'Suggestions' and her other holds a *'pass the plate.'*

She awakens. Time to dive into links sent by the librarian.

LUMINSTRATUM

Blue Clear Skies behind David Anthony and My Lady.

My Lady: You know many cultures and religions have rules and ideas about spirituality and so-called languages - with a word for 'messenger spirit' and 'ministering spirit'. Exponentiates when adding their synonyms.

David Anthony: My entity no longer sleeps, I haven't dreamt in eight years. No eyes to close, I see without them! Isn't it wonderful to be without matter?

My Lady: Your attitude about body switches around too much! I am recognizing more things about Mary's personality. And Rhetta's here, she needs to relax and let it come to her. All have good humor, great discussions. Seems there are levels of life and spirit and afterlife which they are not as aware of as we are.

David Anthony: Of course. How much did we know about the planet matter? Energies linger where no human sees. All are affected by what's around them. I understand that this PNW area was affected while it formed, being split and spit as a flare by the equator of their sun.

My Lady: Nine revolving planets and one's a bit off balance. Most have at least one moon. Jupiter has 80 and Saturn has 83, its biggest is called Titan. Moons control emotions. Says the lore here, people interpret the cosmos.

David Anthony: Galaxies collide. Elements scatter to land, different bodies accompany spinning matter, the spinning have rhythm and speed, and detachment. This area encountered to long ago with collision. Another reason we were sent to see and monitor their reaction to all this.

Chapter THREE

Monday a.m. August 3rd, WVC

Mary woke several times before dawn on Monday, scrambling to remember anything. Where are we and what is this place called? Mike hadn't returned, or had he? A traumatic cloud. She once read stories of others going through trauma.

One arm ached a tad less, or she was acclimating. Or nerves died. Her feet felt nothing. Maybe they'll get chopped off.

So, she whispered to no one, "yay! I'm alive."

Her state of gratitude breaks when the memory of Meghan's sweet face appears. Her dear girl was scheduled to return from camp. This week! She imagined Meghan's puzzled desperate eyes looking around. Where was her mom? Mary then switched her focus, pleading to the universe: please rescue us!

Only the bars Mike had left by her pillow were fueling her. Her stomach growled louder than ever. Maybe that's why the squirrel just scooted beneath a bush.

Where, oh where is Mike?

Last night's weird dream needed to be Squib recorded, but she recollected. Her fruitless search last night to locate her Squib Book meant digging deeper for a breakfast cola in the side pocket of her bag just to get caffeine. Aha! the Squib Book was in the second side pocket of the bag waiting for her. Lo, relief!

The identically placed disorder was unmoved throughout the night - leaning toward evidence Mike hadn't returned. His tools lay atop his bag with a tomato juice can. Same way.

Warm cola gave caffeination and she soon perkily analyzed what she'd dreamt last night. Pencil in hand with a clear short-term memory, she squibbed quickly to not lose any of it:

'Age ten, parents still married, we all cradled a bumpy cleavage of tree branches, Dad read to us. Funny, but not funny, Dad, in the dream, had his same voice but his face was Dave's, [David Anthony's face when living]. One border station was being built and builders captured wild illegal immigrants. If agreeable to sterilization they'd be housed and trained, Mother tore branches off to build homes then pitched small twigs at the officers. Like dreams do, the scene shifted, parents argued. Angst-filling scenes.

Did that imagery originate due to yesterday's trauma? Watch out, brain neurons might have rearranged. Intricate networks. She sleepily and suddenly remembered all she'd felt when Meghan was months from being born, and the embarrassment and sadness in how her fiancé Dave and his buddies had been in trouble at his business, and we being sued.

After being let go from college, he'd designed an 'intimate talks' phone business. One woman had become emotional then hurt, so retaliated. David's defense was it helped women. That was the year Mary took up Squibbing, and the year he had died.

"Mike!" She calls out. No trace, no response. She looks at the bowl and spoon he'd left for her. She holds the spoon to bang the bowl a few times. Stupidly muffled, it didn't alarm the critters to scatter. No movement, no response. More worrisome unrest.

She is worried, the sun is way too hot. Sweating on top of this misery. Where's aspirin? He must be hot and thirsty. Is he lost? Collapsed somewhere? What will she do next?

"**Help!** It's all sooo *bad here, please!*" She surprises herself, bends her knees, sobs, prays. "Someone, brave it, brave that slivered detour!"

Doubt, like a bad habit, flees from keeping any morsel of faith. What if Mike doesn't return? She pleads to any good power. If he doesn't, she'd need to heal fast to walk all those miles to the highway – before food runs out. So animalistic, dizzy and sick.

Limping miles without a map? She can't move today.

Planes or drones patrolling? Only large white birds. Do they notice irregularity? Capable of reading people? If they could, they'd likely ditch this place.

Hunger causes her head to ache. More bars? He couldn't have walked too far – with such pain! She calculates Aug 2 –

Nov 30, approximately 121 days for meals – the amount he'd planned for himself, only, it was to be all his, nobody else's.

She hadn't packed food, of course. Her eating his would deduct and broadcast inequity of her noncontributions. She'd need to defend herself with *'I planned on reunion food, supposedly feeding me. Fair, that I eat some of yours. Being stuck wasn't my doing.'*

"I didn't make a bad turn!" she shouts out - to anyone.

Silence.

Memories of scarcity emerge, like her father's sudden parenthood to five step-kids, due to the new marriage of a newly pregnant bride. Mary was forcibly led into a room by the woman, "Don't even hint for money over what your mom is already getting for you in monthly for child support."

Power imbalances. Who has the stash of food, the gold? So many mouths to feed? Shouldn't prospective parents take a test or grasp math before nesting, before procreating? Hadn't they figured out how dollies would eat? Would they want trendy stuff, clothes, pets and parties? Become sick? Mary barely covered expenses with a good job and one good child.

A shovel load of hyper alert fear poured into her heart, imagining more *what ifs*. No new tire tracks were made last night.

Reverse that direction, she ordered herself. For eight years she'd been raising her daughter alone. Meg was smart when handling uncertainty. Resourceful. Emergency lists were in big, bold letters, taped throughout their home.

Dear Lord. Mike wouldn't let her starve. Those imbalances of worth morphed ill will at times, especially between genders.

Other than the Grand Faux detour choice and a meandered research style, he had sensibility - but misplaced it yesterday!

82

Now, how again was it decided to join up together for this trip? Where to place the blame? This 'coupling' supposedly for only ten hours on a highway? Traditional male/female space sharing? Oh, don't take advantage of that term. *Oh…that!* Dear Lord, why be focusing on *that?* No more venturing *there!* They were professional humans -- not primarily defined as genders, sexes!

He'd not once expressed the slightest curiosity about her personal life. Being carefully aloof? Flawed? *'Yes, I am burdened by archaic role assumptions!'* She would remind him when he returned.

Whose fault was this? This wrecked-van camp. This WVC.

She quickly writes, *'Besides, the photograph of the young blond girl, yes, it indicates an evidence record of involvement -- does that blonde do any research? Does she have a printer? A degree? Oh, wait, this isn't a competition. You're not interested in him anyway. Remember, and he isn't either. It's the subscription passwords! Oh. Duh, me.'*

Insects, heat, pain! Crippled! Reverence here, she breathes. Stop borrowing more trouble, she prays. Rid illusions, stop the fear. Clout means nothing here, clout doesn't matter here. She squibbed: *'…dwindled power now, you're without research ability. The password goldmine lost its leverage, vanished!'*

Where's the rescue? Oh, dear God, how much longer?

Fast Forward December 21, 2020 - Inside a Lodge

Out of the window of the cozy lodge the two see it's snowing. The fireplace cradles heat. The couple take in closeness and relish the dancing orange and yellow fire, casting shadows.

It's a search now, important. Professor and/or Dr. Michael Merrick's profile is nearly in the hands of five detectives. Another page, yes, he is for real, get the search in order, quick! Focus!

Concentrate. READ ALL OF THIS. Immediacy is the command.

The words within my professional vocabulary aren't adequate to describe last night's occurrence. Not now. My entire experience is a new concept, a mere dilemma due to lack of distinct synonyms, but like any language, inefficiency results when trying to speedily communicate. Meaning and truth are diluted. The total experience has no words. No qualifying consensus so no assigned words for 'it'.

Chimes! Sort of, but no. Whatever they were, they did soothe, took my pain totally away – while they sounded. Perhaps bells? An iron bell? Not as deep or strong as the carillon, but tingly though not shrill, metals in instruments have combinations of elements like brass, copper, aluminum. Nothing ever before is what I heard last night, though. Structured with undefined material? Nothing I heard was purely string, purely wind, or percussion.

Let me add here, since the world's collective intelligence is not even slightly aware, there are trillions of galaxies in our known universe, and we sure don't know enough regarding their compositions or their loosened and shot off elements. Indescribability means a delayed consensus! Yes, yes, I know that AI will create

music. Well, if I'm magically bestowed even a
player near the cave, I will return to edit this.

Sections of the WVC boomerang the sun's blare. Yards away he spots Mary's head bop up and down; she's a limping tempo. Had she just yelled his name? He refocuses to affirm he'll lock the hill experience into his personal mystery vault.

But first, find a business bush!

Crouching and spying through branches he notes the feathers' lustrous patterns haven't been disturbed. The precision is intricate. More than when seeing them moonlit.

Their weave pattern surpasses those of dragonfly wings.

The deer are not there now, but the owl remains.

When rescuers arrive, Mike thinks they'll be made certain to clean and bag the wings. Think positive.

Homesickness crawls in his heart, Mike aches for his pets to levy power for turns to snuggle. If his dog had accompanied him instead of Mary, no awful detour would have been sought. He'd still have a pristine van. He wouldn't be here.

Mary again wrestles with the should haves. She should have flown, as originally planned. What brought them into this pairing? Had she been secretly holding a clear, desireful image to couple with him? Had he thus designed 'them' while driving together?

Duh, again. '*…he bought a fancy van. The passwords and van, since then, have BOTH lost worth.*'… '*a frog who chose a detour only wide enough for a frog! He owns now a lot of strewn items, food, and a spanking new wrecked luxury van! The frog has deserted me.*'

'*All his fault. Words HE'D said, like, I realize what I am not good at it.*' *And I recently learned a few things that he didn't know already!*' Her teeth began to grind.

A gravelly grating beyond the trees becomes clearer and then much louder, nearing. She grabs a knife, jolting the pain in her arm, then stiffens in the case it's not Mike or the rescuers.

All at once, every bit of anger's degradation dissipates when she sees his face clearly, it's bruised, banged. He looks horridly precious in the sun's light. Her layered resolve and arguable artillery peels away. She softens, simply wanting to offer healing.

Also feeling the dissonance of relief that there won't be vultures circling about him, nor will she stumble with aches and pains while walking and calling out his name any more to find him – no tripping over or on his injured or dead, decaying body.

Off balance, he limps. His bruised head and kind, blue eyes complain with glints of pain. He refuses aspirin. Then he accepts her dampened towel and mumbles thanks in a whisper.

He doesn't look bad enough to die soon, and there's food. Here she is, already preparing something for him to eat and drink!

"Mary! Ever learn that owls have incredibly superior eyesight? Magnificent compared to a human's ability to detect light and movement! Humans are gypped. A lot we can't see!"

He doesn't look at her, or at anything. His mind is alone, spinning. "Their retinas excel with a huge ratio of rods for every cone. They're superb, those owls, seeing movement in the dark!"

Mary is transfixed. He's like an idiot. "I don't need improved retinas to see the horror. You're beat up, spent! You shake! What's going on? What happened last night?"

"Mary, I saw huge white crapped-upon feathers. Maybe torn from a huge bird. I mean HUGE, BEAUTIFUL!" She squints. Her own image of 'huge wings' is they are of an angel's.

After a few bites of apple and peanut butter, he clears his

throat, "There's a wrecked helicopter with dead bodies in it."

She gasps, chokes in disgust.

Both agree to soon respond. Plan first aid – in case victims weren't yet completely gone. But her hips won't carry her, nor will her arms lift or support another body, dead or alive.

"Were there flies on the bodies?"

"Didn't see. Likely they died yesterday or last night."

"If they're indeed dead, why just let them decompose?"

"Can't lift, then can't bury."

"Will they smell?"

"Don't know."

"Who are they?"

Are they important? Important enough?

Mike volleys between his condition and the copter. He revisits the hill sounds, then begins elocuting every single experience, but saves to shut his lips. Don't *ever* tell Mary, he thinks. *Too many anomalies exponentiate, and I am clueless.*

He wants to bury his head, preferably in a faraway study.

Mary says, "Maybe drag the dead somehow? Slowly? Or leave them until the rescuers can drag?"

"Wear your pandemic mask, they might emit gases."

He'd once shared with Mary how the strength of his cadaver revulsion ended his medical doctor major.

Mary stops from asking if the copter held anything useful for them to use. It is an insensitive thought, but practical.

He is there, "Hoping cells are in the copter, ones picking up a signal. Better, valuables like a workable transponder!"

She's grateful he speaks for both. Grimacing, they gather first-aid cases, a small shovel, then a rope to tie on an emptied plastic tub handle, "decomposing scents quickly reach animals."

Another gravelly sound of dragging approaches and grows louder. Then a scraping sound. Grunting, whining.

Are rescuers here at last? Hurrah!

Yellow Pad Found December 21, 2020.
Professor Merrick. p/7 of 52 (8/3/20)

From the WVC, I need to be out by 9 p.m. to record. Am using an extra cell phone. Foreign words and other sounds hum indistinctly through the night, emitted either from throats of fauna, the rubs of flora, or are carried by mild winds to hit cave walls? Emitted from some very foreign being, or from other unknown parts of the universe(s)?

Our university voted once to rename a department to be 'World Languages.' It was formerly named 'Foreign Languages.' English only speakers had with arrogance considered 'other' languages as 'foreign.' (Diversity advocates, therefore, 'world languages.' meant becoming 'all languages inclusive'). Cultures' languages communicate concepts and need their processes. Etymology and dictionaries sought much effort with existing builds of systems. Complex indexing and transferable labeling endure a time-consuming consensus!

A challenging, multi-cultural populus exists today. That issue was one study planned for my sabbatical, but an incorrect detour choice had cast me here. (Unless connectivity is restored, and we get rescued.) I refer to the camping hill base as 'Detourist Cave.'

The Fallow on August 3rd, Near Tijuana, Mexico

Within the week Dena would be receiving a newly announced, trial treatment, either while in Los Angeles or Santa Barbara – a top-notch nursing home would administer. Rudolf would either stay on the yacht or at their Montecito home.

Dena remained optimistic about current progress and believed she'd get better. But something else big tugged at her.

All three kids noted 'how much.' No deep dives of ever questioning themselves with 'why.' How much did they own, want, what did their friends earn, how much more out there to get…. They simply felt entitled and therefore deserved more.

Too often, now, she'd be fatigued, weak, then rise. Seconds later she'd sit back down. Her deck chair wasn't cozy. They preferred she'd stay in bed - then they'd freely speak without hearing her opinions, unwanted advice, uninteresting tidbits. Like adolescents, they felt she didn't 'get it.' And somehow, it mattered not how they knew, they just knew it all.

All three of them were a few years away from thirty. How quickly her babies had grown and now were often strangers to her. Less than two decades ago, before letting big money taint simpleton happiness, she'd stated she'd not ever shop for things

89

like a curved loofa cushioned sofa. Now they sat on them surrounding both yachts' custom-made fire pits.

The Marcher family cuddled together at one time while sitting on lawn blankets enjoying a tiny patio's $17 BBQ, eating s'mores. They'd rinse sticky fingers using the tract home's garden hose while the dog helped eat droppings off the lawn

No maids then, nor assistants. Today, seven personal staff attended. Her children sneered, the yachts 'were old and predictable.' The old sun and moon no longer provided wonderful effects. 'Desensitization' wasn't in their vocabulary.

Only Dena and Rudy enjoyed the gorgeous sunsets.

The kids anxious for newness never hid boredom.

So, what if Dena was suffering, with thoughts of dying? It wasn't substantial enough, she wasn't gasping on her death bed, why go there? With no personal experience having anyone close to them die, all they focused upon was their phones or how much this cruise was taking away their time. This excursion up the Pacific Coast was something they'd already done too many times. Borrrring.

Minutes after signing their driver's licenses, on their 16th birthdays, each drove off in a gifted, fully equipped car. No "should" be grateful about anything, it's quite okay and comfortable that 99 % of the world can't imagine a life so grand. Why should anyone be concerned? Focus on richest winners, not the poorest losers. Their reality.

Dena's strength lessened, and she couldn't stand for too long, the Halbert's often reminded her: "Don't walk with soft shoes, Mrs. Marcher, the *Fallow* floors are the waxiest!" *The Fallow* was a dear family heirloom, the oldest yacht of all three. Having the sturdiest gear. Increasingly, Dean looked forward to a comfortable bed at a very caring care home, and off the yacht.

WVC August 3rd, Nearly Lunchtime

A pair of orange and blue shoes with rope tied on each ankle stumbled into the WVC, pulling a dragging dark-skinned busty woman on a makeshift sled-sleeping bag. Her braided three-layered dyed hair is twisted atop her bobbling head. She's being yanked over various rocks and wood chunks.

She's sneering. Very white teeth bite her over-plumped up bottom lip. She draws in others' stunned attention. Mary notes a loosened fake eyelash on her chin. Tattoos are on both.

Invasion of living corpses! Amazement mixes with loathing. With these two, nothing becomes easier. With honed practice, Mike classifies segmented socioeconomics, education, and ethnicity. He'd record quietly and proceed to filter with appropriate scientific questioning, trying out more variables.

Thickened make-up, lashes, stiffening shots, nose rings, and tattoos were rampant. Mike's multicultural group of colleague scholars would eventually hear and read his take of this. Nothing would surprise them, and Professor Merrick knew to shed bias before write-ups.

Mary wonders why a woman decorates herself for a man she appears to despise. The lady's other loosened lash is stuck to her ear. One earring is gone. She darts a harsh glance at Mary.

Sweat pours off the man. His eyes glare at Mary or don't meet her eyes, shifting back and forth. The woman's facial muscles appear frozen. These two beings show through their eyes how tired, famished and thirsty they are.

Sucking his breath, the man dizzyingly lands face down, at Mary's feet. Reflexing to break his fall, she hurts herself. Gathering, he brushes himself off then eyes water bottles. The woman says she's hungry, though also hasn't made eye contact. They smell bad and she painfully digs inside her bag for a mirror.

"Already are seeing how you look," Mary offers, "because grooming could become handy when the savior busses arrive to rescue. We thought you were it. You aren't. Disappointments haven't ceased. Care to introduce yourselves?"

Mike shows Mary a 'be careful' signal with his eyes and facial expression. She knows what he means.

Names follow. It takes ten minutes. Jude. For the seventh time today, Mary's fingers habitually reach toward her online keypad. Her aim is to search for people-find. Taming a new habit, sans a keyboard, still isn't registering. She screeches.

She sucks in a deep breath, piercing her lungs again.

Neither Juniper hears Mike and Mary introduce themselves. Janna's in her mirror again and Jude is slapping flies off sweaty legs. Both wrestle with their anxieties.

Janna darts a look toward 'that judging lady,' who probably likes book-wormy, snippy, stuffy stuff, feels superior. And now that lady jots everything with a pencil. She squints. A lot. No wonder wrinkles are forming on her eyes and forehead.

Everyone's bruises blare. That lady, is her name Mary? Her glasses won't conceal darker bruises. She's probably single and frigid. She has nice teeth, though, without caps.

In a moment she will offer Mary tips how to fix that hair, lose the glasses, get some color on her eyes and her lips, then get surgery in a few years. At least shots.

Mary loathes. How will she and Mike rid them? Her lack of compassion is from her anger, and she admits it. The guy, Jude, looking straight in her face now, sneers at her when seeing her expression.

Mike sizes-up that the Junipers are comparatively resourceless and will no doubt expect his food. More dread to add. No care, no awareness, no plan, seemingly no curiosity as both don't ask questions and look around for ten minutes.

After 14 minutes of wordless gorging and hydrating, Jude sits silently on a lawn chair, assessing both. They are smart, or think they are, and that banged up lady is snooty, distant, a bore. Not mainstream. They probably don't like web games, alcohol, drugs or music or parties.

This will be so horrible if we're not out of here soon – all four thought the same thing.

Mary hopes her Meggie won't ever pierce or tattoo. Jude sees Mary noting, with a sour expression, his array of skin art. Her upper lip is trying not to sneer.

"Hey – what is your name? Mary?"

"Mary Hawkings."

"Tattoos on my arm, these here." He taps his forearm and shoulder, "you're hardly camouflaging your snotty sneer, your Highness, Mary. Carlos Castenada said we all should balance our terror of being alive with the wonderment of it. That is why this tattooed angel on my arm is holding a shield. The angel's other hand holds heart shaped spectacles. Look deeply. Be cool. You show you think you're better than Janna and me. A snob."

Mary doesn't want the label, nor see herself this way and is embarrassed. She vows immediately to be kind but has to say her piece before peace is made.

"Beyond being unattractive – at least, for myself, I think tattoos are nonsensical. Tastes change if one reaches maturity.

If you live to realize your tattoo is undecipherable, it's because its canvas has wrinkled. And they're costly to remove. Horrible on old skin. One might not live long to see that, though, since tattoos associate also with poor health habits and drug use.

"Soften this!" Mike is alarmed by her valor.

Jude shows he isn't surprised.

"Hey, all, this banter must cease! Learn about each other! We don't know a great thing about each other to fix opinions or achieve a consensus. Talk other topics." Mike offers.

There's good news, though. Mary is grateful the others aren't dead. Only because there won't be vultures or decay. No lifting or burying. Mike and she won't rupture body parts or feel squeamish breathing their stench - sweat and alcohol.

Pick a poison. Attempted positivity fails each minute. She sighs, says to herself to 'give them a graceful break, Mary.'

They've not been born as lucky, a first compassionate check point, Mike whispers. She tries to correct her attitude. But truly, how would anyone venture out in an unsafe helicopter for something named 'Behind the Avatar' party?

Cookies are offered. The two grab to eat, chewing and yapping with their mouths full. Minutes later, with a new sugar high, they're slapping the bugs on them, to suck upon sweaty skin. Mike estimates they're 30 years old. Topics to discuss?

"Mike took a wrong turn yesterday to meet two falling trees. Explains having your copter crashing on trees." Mike decides to fade out, escape this. But the good part is they're all in too poor shape to physically hurt each other.

In just a few, off to the hill base. Realizing his blatancy and unfairness to leave Mary with them, he could gather strategic forethought. He tells himself to build defense if accused of selfishness.

Janna gabs on. She's a self-professed expert on make-up shades, styling, shaping, chemical peels. Mary never dyed her hair. Janna limps over to study Mary's epidermis. Mary is too tired to care, wants Janna to shut her mouth, her breath stinks.

Jude claims he's selling to high end buyers, always sketching, planning, dreaming. He asks if they both buy art.

Only baseball for Mike, Mary speaks. For herself, "I am a follower of classic art prints."

"So, you don't like original work? I figured. Yeah, plenty of people are like rusty bolts and screws - what we call tight wads, the kind who won't shop at fairs."

"Not into rusty bolts. After your statement, I'm not impelled to see what you've made." Mary is weary, "Plan to go back to the copter tonight? Please note we aren't a hotel, Jude."

Mike weighs again when to dart off toward his second hill visit. A lecture on functional perspective vs conflict perspective from him right now? NO. They'd not grasp it. This was an interesting watch, though. Peculiar group.

And likely odd, new variables will pop up to surprise.

Jude is aware he's transgressed. "We can't fit comfortably in the copter. Full of pain. You guys into pain killers?"

Janna strikes a bold pose and now advises, "hair high-lightening is what you, Mary, might like -- at least five years ago!" Then laughs a bit nervously at Mary's cold sneer.

Mary bristles. "You must know I've better things to do with my time and money than cover with fake veneers. I try not to focus on decorating myself. Been there. It's a disorder, and it's best not to hide. It could compromise one's mental health."

She shakes her head and looks deeply at Janna's eyes, not quite into them, they're so blackened and guarded.

Janna involuntarily drops her mirror.

Mary confirms no talking social issues. They'd be futile. They're poorly read, would parrot junk. Probe rescue ideas.

Jude says, "honking the van's horn, set trash on fire?"

"I need to rest," Mary feels heavier homesickness for her cozy home, a simple life of cable and e-books, fireplaces, and a windowsill. All seem like a princess castle. Missing the library.

Mike vanished from sight, he'd limped off.

Janna wonders if the two sleep together, are a unit.

Heads turn to see Mike hobbling back from the mere 10 yards he'd made progress on reaching, to fetch his yellow pad, recorder, a few apples. Now he hears the Junipers start in about their inheritance. Whining follows. They'd missed the meet-up.

"Do keep the chatter low or go back to the helicopter to talk, please," Mike orders. "Notice how Mary is trying a short nap?" Then, Mike raises his decibels like an instructor would demand order. "Did you two pack food besides cheese, crackers, wine or vodka? What else might be on your short list? Have you anything helpful or nourishing?"

The Junipers describe how some wine shattered but vodka and rum were fine. Jude's eyes widen, "Hey, man, we're all hurtin' a lot here an' all. Sheesh! Look at all what's happening. Hey, chill, man. This campsite mood needs lifting. Get high."

Hours later, Mary squibs about Jude, being one to watch.

96

'Muddled from narcotic use and probably been reared by poorly prepared parents, reluctant readers with bad habits, patterns. More time would tell.'

Mary decides to hold tighter to hope. Please! A rescue would end this. The social psychologist role wasn't her lane, and she begins to Squib again. *'I need cases to read. I need support. Will wing it while I am here. It must be sooner, not later, that we're rescued!'*

Then she crosses her heart.

Yellow Pad Found December 21, 2020.
Professor Merrick. p/11 of 52, (8/4/20)

Building and planning a field test isn't simple. Research scientists first attempt to identify and understand each nuance of their research question. Next, they appropriately proceed to prepare set up. They study every change within a decipherable baseline (collection of consistent data) which fluctuates according to how the variables are planned. Groups of samples are needed for testing a formed hypothesis, based on observation. Randomizing participants and setting controls for confounding variables are involved. I must say here right now that absolutely nothing is consistent, nor do I recognize anything. The sound of music must be of instruments from another world. What makes those sounds, I still question. How is it euphoric? I have no test ready. I don't know what I am doing. Nothing is a defined variable, nothing, nothing, nothing labeled. I can't note consistency. Must there be? That is a fair question. To integrate any possibility for a designated 'base line.' I am stupefied.

Being consistently without connectivity since detouring is unhelpful. Given that my discipline is social psychology, there's unlikelihood I can succeed because first, nothing sounds the same in any visit, it is all too random. Why can't I see them? From where did/do they originate and how were they built, executed? Again, and most importantly, "they" needs to be defined.

WVC - August 9th, 2020

After six days of groaning discomfort, only slight physical improvement is notable. It's the sunshine and beauty beyond the WVC, the clean air and vibrant colors which slightly help improve the campers' dispositions. The pine smell and smoky campfires invite ambiance.

Mary thinks its electrolytes, maybe neutrinos, maybe faith. Only three out of eight arms aren't piercing in pain. A total of eight limping legs and four bruising torsos won't heal if lungs can't painlessly inhale enough oxygen for walking very far. Mike has begun calculating and rationing out food.

They've shed denial and shock as each awakened to their separately processed, altered reality. Grunts and complaints don't cease. Simplicity becomes the rule over seeking joyfulness

To get along, the Junipers realize rules have reasons. Monitored mostly by Mary, led by Mike, they wear kid gloves and have announced the campsite needs each to follow every rule.

First, do not smell bad. Second, maintain tidy areas. Between the hours of dawn to dusk, each are to "will" use times from the communal heated water. It will be simmering from the campfire's large boiling-pot. Use separate pouring bowls. Cool the water prior to rinsing bare skin. While cleaning, stand behind named labeled trees. Do not run around without wearing clothes. Keep your shoes near or on.

Jude sings made up songs while washing. Most tunes are adlib made up and hilarious, others are crude. Janna shares showers and they stay a long time because of torn muscles. They vibrate colorful innuendos. WVC audience amusement is born.

Whenever Janna pours rinse water over him, they both turn, sometimes sliding and slipping on each other, hurting themselves and not holding back the pained shouts. All is amplified. Next, he will pour her. Groans sound harmonious at times, and this brings levity to their scrubbing episodes.

Mary and Mike each shower solo using soap-free sponges. She cleans with lemon and vinegar, then puts petroleum jelly on her skin. Each holds an ear out for the other while bathing in case rescuing a slip and fall is needed. Mary prefers that Janna, a woman, is more willing to act as a standby, but that's not the case and is extra slow and careful showering alone.

It's a bit chilly by midnight, and essential to dry towels on the line during the day. Mike's packed clothespins work well. But he wonders how long the bar soap will last, how to distribute dishes, extra pillows, petroleum jelly, toothpaste.

In return, Mike firmly yet politely and loudly announces he is excused from fishing the brook, he won't be a food hunter. They readily vote whether to agree in fairness. All affirm it.

They must get better if they are not rescued soon.

WVC August 12, 2020

Mary offers two pairs of nylon panty hose (she'd packed

for the reunion). This will trap small freshwater fish swimming downstream. All are extremely grateful for the brook.

"Place the nylon's panty part, the crouch, to neck's nape to securely hold it. Separate the two leg parts which are filled with screen-trapped fish. Fills will bounce. Stay put walking back in a slow crawl. Two at a time, take turns."

"Continue thinking practically."

Mike has trouble stopping his laughter, it hurts his ribs.

"There's not enough packed food for four. We all know the dilemma. No surviving on what I'd planned for just myself. No traffic has shown its halo on our path. We will fish every single day. Then freeze them. Should slingshots be made to kill birds and mammals?"

He continues, "Nightly walks are supposed to be good. Painful, though. Stay alert of ones that would love to eat you!

"I think I'll build sling shots. Have any big rubber bands? I will need screws and drivers and wood sticks." Jude starts to joke about the screws, innuendo form.

Hours later, sipping lemon water, Mary spots Janna and Jude waddling back from the stream, grimacing. Both stop every seventh step, a cumbersome sight, wobbling a bouncing bounty of silver fish stuffed in a nude-toned nylon panty hose. They lean on tree barks, then regroup.

Closing in, Janna's tears, grunts, is pitied. Removing the panty portion from her neck will take three of them, muffling their cries. One swoop, each fist grasps nylon, then heaves it off her neck. Quickly it is turned so the panty opening faces the readied wax paper. The slimy silver is poured, all slither freely.

Not an appetizing image, nor smell, and all walk from it. No offers are made for cleaning or exchanging recipes.

Mary is repulsed, not feeling like eating the wiggly silver things. Her agenda is to dodge this responsibility. Not to be blamed if the final fish dish tastes horrible. Mike looks forward to chili beans and crackers tonight. But he chimes, "Let's bag them and freeze 'um!"

The Junipers' faces glow with pride through their sweat. Mike schedules the next trip, then offers a high five gratitude signal using his better arm. Mary's Squib Book receives words describing *'yellow, blue and brown bruises and silver slime today.'*

"The freezer should stay full always! A lot of walks to and from the brook!" And while trekking, check the condition of the feather pile. Exercise is physical therapy. Splinted bones, twists and sprains and punctures will heal!

"Nursing fractured thoughts."

"Praying for better mind processing. I mean, look at us! If you don't mind."

"Yea, nobody in their right mind would be here."

Mike continues the pun, "If we had tastebuds like a catfish or a regular octopus that we'd pick up every single taste there is. Do you mind if we experience other flavors?"

"How's that? We can't taste all the flavors now?"

"It's lack of some buds. We've 10,000 taste-sensitive cells compared to others in the animal kingdom with 150,000."

Mary places her fork down hard. Her nose wrinkles. She looks at her fish and frowns. "Lately *I love* the taste of ketchup, sugar, a squirt of lemon and pepper. My buds are underdeveloped, I suppose. And I don't care. And what reason

101

does the Maker provide us with lack for that? Does sense of smell factor in?" Mary darts, feeling repulsed each second.

Mike smiles, "Catfish nearly tops again there! Olfactory tissues with fewer than 100 folds in most living vertebrates, but catfish have more than 140."

For 20 minutes, their conversation centers on new ideas and objects and 'stumbled upon' knowledge. A bit of scientific study and peer reviewed processes are added. He is aware this is elementary but sees they're inspired to listen closely.

Scientific planning was of utmost importance; Mike tried to explain. Eyes began gazing and drooping too soon for his liking, he realized, but he took glee from the little success.

A sliver of their interest, Mike smiles, "See? Without computers, tv's, or phones! Hours of verbal exchange! Thumbs up to bare-boned environments! Constructive conversation!"

"But allow a fly in this syrup! All this is ample unchecked exchange!" Mary laughs, "fact checking capacity is not here!"

Janna, sweating, tries smiling as she turns from the smell. She's not hungry, wants to sleep, muscles ache worse than they did yesterday, she'd explained. "A little fever, but sure I will see you in the morning." It was four p.m. As soon as her head hit the pillow, she was out. Mike wonders about Covid relapse.

Mary daydreams home tasks -- finishing and starting when returning home. Her stomach aches imagining Meghan searching. Maybe Gracie's mother, Mrs. Land, is with her now. Her throat swells. Tears travel behind her sunglasses. She reminiscences about wanting a husband who'd be very handy, especially now. She remembers Dave. She silently prays.

Nobody notices. By now, the university library would be noting her absence. Likely, there hasn't yet been an emergency issuance since it's still summer break for most. Has anyone knocked on her front door after failing to reach her? Who is in the library right now? Student workers? Adjuncts?

Mike tacks up another list of rules on a wooden stump: *Clean each separate business bush afterward. Take care of your wipes — No tissue so use leaves, bark, rocks. Roll them on the ground to clean them, then pour thick cover like a cat, this will help detracting insects or animals with stench. Use plasticware and your bag to dispose of it.'*

Janna decorate with markers to label her bags, and others follow suit — results are silly, fringing crudity and dark humor.

Mike is checking the labels on empty subscription pain killer cannisters he found in the Juniper's trash. What did baseball players do prior to tablet form aspirin? Had the American League honored willow bark? Who was the synthesizer of salicin? He continued to review baseball glory, quizzing himself, and decides to suddenly to skip the cave for a night to focus on rubbing menthol on his calves and arms.

Limbs ache. Planning pain interruption includes avoiding direct pressure on injuries. Shorter spans of sitting still. Mary starts laughing, imagining her chair at the library, sitting on her feet. Her knees can't bend like that anymore.

The next day, Mike and Jude design and construct a lounge chair out of emptied plastic storage tubs, shaped and cushioned, with wadded, taped towels. "Mary can sleep on this. One of us might help retape towel bundles…now and then."

LUMINSTRATUM *Clear Skies behind David Anthony and My Lady.*

David Anthony: *Tell me the truth, My Lady…I shouldn't have phrased it this way… since knowing that you are the essence of truth, otherwise you wouldn't have made it to here.*

My Lady:	About my knowledge of earth type planets?
David Anthony:	All people were born with a mission, and the maker distinctly provided each person with theirs. I will talk about becoming a celestial minister full of love and compassion. Help them with that? Looks more like they need physical healing. My Lady, I need to ask. Did you want this?
My Lady:	Not even in my dreams did I think of myself without matter and would become this, doing all this! Checking collisions! Let's keep alert about RIGHT NOW.
David Anthony:	We will find out…. And spiders dream, and monkeys tease, and otters hold hands. At least they do on earth. And I love you, my celestial mate, my dear, kind lady.

WVC - August 14th, 2020

"Look, more whistles!" Mike empties a lunch bag full of shiny hunter's red and blue whistles. He points to where he's headed, "When help arrives or when to scare off the animals! Don't stop blowing them until I'm back at this sorry camp."

He hobbles and waves. Mary has titled these sessions away from them as his 'dusk calling'.

Yellow Pad Found December 21, 2020.
Professor Merrick. p/17 of 52 (8/14/20)

I comprehend differences between imagination and my overall ability to evaluate. This involves ranges of tangibility and common sense of sight touch, and sound. I have difficulty understanding tiniest nuanced differences. There's an increase in discernable words, I'm acutely tuning, aa vague still of context. My faith is being fed. It is mine.

In yesterday's base hill cave darkness, for

104

seconds, I noted a tiny dim glow hover in the vicinity of where the 'music' sounded. It ceased too soon. No better description. Maybe later.

WVC - August 15th, 2020

He waited until sunrise to leave the hill base because he wanted to check on the feathers. And it was quiet in the cave last night. No activity had occurred, no sight or sound, and this morning's wings filled him. They struck awe every single time.

Three sets of sleepy eyes barely register his slow entry into the WVC. Mary has set trays. She'd discovered tan cloth napkins he'd packed; they brought a civilized beauty to the table, and she centered pieced leaves and wildflowers in a vase.

She's speaking less and is worse at moving without loud whimpering, sometimes shrieking. Her bruising isn't healing. One arm hangs completely useless at her side, twice she's tried sewing an operative sling, is stooping. Her eyes show resignation and tears behind sunglasses.

"I don't know where you go or why each night, Mike. Your face shows you know something that I don't."

"I do see a lot, Mary. What I learn is hard for me to talk about at this point. I am recording things."

In the next cave visit he hears a tone, a timbre like a bird's whistling. It is a soft bellowing, echoing chirp.

He asks the others later, "Do you know some dinosaurs likely sounded like birds? Scientists' similarities in larynx-like cartilages inside both creatures."

"I guess it's interesting to you. It's Yawn-Ville here. To you, respectfully, sorry," Janna says, bothered and grouchy.

105

"*Larynxes?* The heck? Or will I ever care to know?"

That stopped Mike's sharing of how dinosaurs evolved from a species less than two feet long to a humungous - 120,000,000 years ago, couldn't feed easily and they died. .

As though three 7 inch long recently overfed lizards suddenly felt vibration from their reptilian class, the trio scurried off the make-shift table, to the ground and raced toward Janna's sleeping bag. She starts screaming.

Mike can't hold back from laughing. Janna takes hold of herself then starts laughing too, then gets off, shakes it and checks inside of it before rolling it up for the day.

She aims an added shot at Mike, "Was your larynx lesson meant for your nerdy bookdragons or birdy behavior classes? Wow. I guess we are supposed to be grateful for finally learning it." She smirks, then smiles, testing Mike.

"Don't run for public office, Janna. Ever."

"Show some respect."

She begins coughing and cannot stop.

"Janna, your symptoms. Think. What do you know about the virus? You've wrestled sickness more than usual?"

"I don't know, all this is unfortunate, isn't it? Just feel like crying. I do cry. A lot. There's no privacy for the injured here. I wish I had my late-night hideaway to visit all night."

Quietly later he wonders about the lizards and if there's a hidden subconscious reason why he hadn't yet ventured in there? Maybe time to share this with others, just to confirm? Would cave performances happen for others?

Instead of talking private thoughts, he speaks loudly,

106

"Wash our face and hands more. Don't touch faces or noses without washing. Sneeze and cough on the back of your wrists!"

Mary adds, "who here would be bringing in any communicable ailment? The critters?"

"Why not just be happy and sing songs around the campfire?" Jude laughs.

"Any suggestions?"

"How about some Beatles 'get back to where you once belong?', Bowie's or Cohen's darker stuff? Anything Pink Floyd or Radio Head? Learning to fly, creep, anything."

"Depeche Mode's 'personal savior' would be good."

Mike digs into his reserve: "In ten days I might be strong to walk the miles to the highway. Strolls are less painful now."

He won't disclose the absolute truth. It's constant pain.

Mary sees how the Junipers' improved alertness and acute pain are due to depleted pain med supply.

"Hey," Jude strums in, "I almost forgot to share this! Ha! Yesterday, out of my jacket pocket, I checked my lottery scratcher! $500 winner! Hey Mike! Whoever can walk out of here the quickest, first hitch a ride to a mini market to cash in!"

"Dumb," Janna laughs. "Meals, gas, hotels, and paying anyone wipes out money. Though maybe exercise your sorry muscles! The calculating areas of your brain, too! Oh, you're smart, you just think we are having a good time being entertained when we're actually laughing at your stupidity."

Jude flexes his muscles, winces to laugh alone at himself.

"That check from your dad's is, I bet, cramming the

mailbox by now. The post office probably is calling the HOA for them to contact us to clear it, make room to get our mail."

"Our fantasy is that we – or I – will be able to pay bills and have money left over to do something grand."

Hope remains for the imminent rescue, Amen.

August 18, 2020 – Gardenia View, Nursing Home

After two years she was the only 25-year-old certified nursing assistant who loved working on Saturdays. Without feigning concern, Shawna focused on the struggling patients.

The hall she loved most was on the third floor. It had been considered "the notched up cushy cushioned" ward at Gardenia View. Several long-term staff, who'd hoped to retire soon, were already overly desensitized by all the plush, over-the-top efforts to impress anyone with big money. Ones sold would weeks later be seen pushing an elderly wheelchaired parent through the entry.

Visitors and the patients' families were scouters. The signees were usually the endeared beneficiaries perfecting their parents' last months. Gardenia implemented new ideas, all the time. Shawna topped that committee, "Gardenia's Sensitizers."

How they catered only to the richest *and* retained its mystique – all were to be custodially happy – at any cost.

Staff were trained to detect the tiniest traces of dissatisfaction. When sadness sept out there was a skilled team assigned to assuage them. Elusive was the state of happiness, that was deeply known, but Gardenia pledged it offered the most pleasant existence until their very end, and all POA's and trust executors monitored their promise.

Famous patients still had it in themselves to be spotlighted and enticing help for better attention. The 'only filthy rich' custodial patients had lived to know how narcissists never benefited others, so remained content with their choice of piped music, warmed custom fitted mattresses, and the world's best doctors. All bedroom windows opened to the east or the west, offering either sunsets or sunrises. Small fireplaces and liquor areas served visitors witnessing a beloved's ending journey.

Dena rested comfortably, narcotic free. Rudolf, on her first day there, had ordered a delivery of five expensive, beautifully carved two-inch high, porcelain fawns nestled beside a taller, perfectly diamond-bladed mother - that's what Shawna saw first.

Shawna saw how gently Dena handled each fawn, smiling, scrutinizing its porcelain details. Soon her focus defaulted on just who had entered her room. Shawna stood out. Outer appearance checkpoints were won over of hair, nails, studded earrings, skin, and overall demeanor. And eye contact.

Her more thorough next check was to evaluate intelligence and attitude. Shawna would be worth studying. This gem would right now, though, be 'get me this or that!'

But add the 'please' kindness. Dena's self-correction arrived. She'd been enlightened by her judgmental patterns, evaluating someone's worth. It was necessary to assess who she could utilize. She now redeemed, feeling the end of her life could be near. She was seeing it in her kids. Enlarged esteem and haughtiness study: Kids of nouveau riche primary adult parents.

How easily Dena commanded another's immediate attention – Shawna noticed how she magnetized. Whatever Dena needed would prompt a load of dispatched calls, help would be instantly rung up. Her goals meant someone's overtime.

Shawna's transparency equated to trustworthiness. She was

very smart. But best, she loved to serve. And in turn, Shawna was in awe of Dena's ability to see right through fools, to diplomatically deal with them, then plan four steps ahead, even in her frail condition.

And to control.

Shawna learned quickly to balance the voice recorder by Dena's lips – personal and legal. Today it was will and trust codicils. Directives. "Make certain my intact lucidity is well documented. Always note with a notary's seal.." Dena tapped a notepad with her long-nailed index finger underneath two names.

"Oh, and Shawna, Shawna is how I am pronouncing it, am I correct? It's not ever to be Shawn or never Shawnie, right? Make sure you ask to speak directly to George, there's his number - gather specifics to ensure this is completed without one flaw."

During breakfast Dena discussed Shawna's mother. Shawna described her mother as having the art of "each present moment to be perceived as perfection. If issues headed south, my mom steered all into a philosophy of Meliorism."

Ceiling lights faded slowly each evening, Dena became awed more often when miniscule lights entered, floating into her room, encircling. As her chosen piped music soothed, the glow evolved, and she began to feel great love, although sure to always scrutinize her water glass for snuck-in traces of calming help. Usually suspicious, often she asked them to empty her glass and in front of her then uncap and pour bottled water.

Yet she always became agitated when thinking of her children.. Having not cared to comprehend the nature of social responsibility, they'd need and deserve to gradually receive less of the dividends. Simple! They'd need to grow and climb with no parents' help, still having more than anyone else would.

Dena's list had causes she was most interested in expanding, including renewable energy, community self-sustenance, education, and health care for the lower middle classes. Rudolf's welfare, if Dena were to die, must be controlled by George's firm of fiduciaries. Also, form a nice home for the elderly – ones not so darned privileged throughout their lives.

Dena negotiated with Gardenia for Shawna to be full time -- with her. They'd strive being on the same, transparent page.

"In the next five years," Dena asked, "if you're with means to achieve it, Shawna, I need to ask you this: what activity is with your visualization? Always your future? What would it take to accomplish?" She inquired how Shawna resolved conflicts.

They agreed: psychological comfort programs to enrich the end of life for each patient with less stress for the family. People shouldn't die penniless or alone, they should die knowing they lived an interesting and good life, and had something to offer the world, just by being within their unit of time. Every patient!"

"Oh, yes, I know you are very wealthy, Mrs. Marcher, but the billionaires should pay their fair share of taxes, I certainly struggle every single day to do so on my level of income!"

"So, what is the monthly income needed for you now?"

Shawna figured it all in a spreadsheet, submitted it to Dena.

Two days later she followed orders to buy Rudolf hats, shirts, stickers, and posters. All were to be embroidered with something containing 'Fawn.' Both smiled over tiny, embroidered words, *'fawners do it with good trouble!'* Inside Dena's note to him, similar to other notes, she wrote, *get fawned on, love, you earned it, you deserve it. Love, D.'*

Chapter FOUR

Mike stays quiet. This must be what affairs could be like. He wasn't levelling but nothing did he have to feel guilt over. He made a vow about nightly jaunts. None needed to know.

He felt a guardian voice say go forward, go deeply. Avoid pre-mature guesswork. Rely and use the scientific process. Allow the struggle to be real. Feel all fully, and with as much new genuine force as possible.

don't conclude anything. Simply gather 'right now.'

Mary retreated daily. Mike tried talking, mostly about her daughter, but she'd step back and keep her head down to focus on meal prepping. With each stir, she clinched her teeth.

They both stood together more often, though. "I need to write. Or read abstracts, am lost, my sad thoughts won't stop."

"Mary, is your Squib book too full?"

While Mike walked from another completely quiet cave visit, he realized these episodes were numbered. Visits would end, either by rescue or his death. If rescued, he would revisit.

It was too surreal and dreamy to completely vanish from his mind and heart. *Would they be there for me always* – was a silly hope. *Of course, eventually I'd have to bring a specialist to witness.* Were they 'just for him' to witness? He laughed at the idea that they were his friends, his childhood glow-in-the dark baseball pals. Still, he was separating imagination from reality. A childish selfishness, he admitted, kept only his, not telling others, hidden on the yellow pads, just for the record. Saving for more.

Thought adjusters from nowhere, it seems, hit him while in plateau moments, out of the blue, like a curve ball. He'd be thinking everything was leveling into copacetic.

A harsh and prickly face-off with last night Mary was still stinging him. He reeled, stayed alone in the cab until hill base time, not shaking off their arrival at drastic odds.

The episode started after dinner. He'd been preparing for the hill base visit when listening to Mary explain to the others about varieties and forms of narcissism. Both had only heard the word a few times. No, she told them, 'Over confidence' and 'liking oneself' is not an illness, it's keeping a healthy image. Voicing one's needs is self-respect. Mary began sharing what she'd written about narcissism in her over-filled Squib Book.

Kindly stating clear boundaries isn't narcissism. Telling someone you deserve to have respect isn't narcissism. She explained the forms of malignant and communal to them. Both were magnetized, full of attention.

Mike offered studies on how lacking empathy hedged toward narcissistic tendencies. "Entitled to break the rules, case study findings." He continued. Experts today are highlighting how narcissists deliberately seek out partners with qualities like empathy, generosity, and optimism — and this was found to be because those traits are easier to exploit, for personal gain."

Mike was gladdened to see their eyes were fascinated.

"Therapy patients had less gray matter in the empathetic parts of their brains."

Both Junipers asked how in the world scientists did these tests. How could anyone ever know so much about all the functions of different parts of the brain or determine which patients to study? And even more inquiries ensued.

"You *all will* learn terms for scientific methods! Mary and you two could learn them soon," Mike was happy with this chat and had paused his hill base visit preps, he was back to the lectern – teach what a controlled test was for, its role, how conducted. When pontificating how all 'should' understand what a theory was, a hypothesis, and types of variables, Mary couldn't hold back. That's when the tornado landed.

Her tone had generated a vibe, increased each second in frequency. "What do you mean, Mike when you say, 'YOU ALL?'" She glared. Her abrupt irritation was loud.

Thus began her whip, her vortex stirred the debris.

"A definition lesson?" Unusually loud and sharp, "I've *already* learned scientific testing terms!" Escalating hotly, she'd been *his* student! Soc Psych 301! He'd obviously forgotten it, she snarled. This hurts. She wanted to throw back the indignance, slam it thickly on him for the night.

Both Junipers heard, the context of it all eluded them.

He hadn't remembered, not at all, not her name, face, or the "A" grades she'd received on term papers.

All this happened years ago! What professor retains names and faces of anyone among forty-other students? The moment final grades were in, bam! Bye! The better looking, funny or brilliant students also vanished from the memory. Soon the next group would shuffle in to learn, test, and leave.

Why had she chosen to suddenly unload all of this?

Signaling refusal to prolong the talk last night, she'd stumbled to her bag by the fire, far from all. Left to ponder what really triggered it, and what else she might be holding on to. Any more stuff to unload, *Mary the minefield?*

He'd sulked for too long. She'd kept all inside and then it

had burst out. His humiliation didn't stop, even when employing favored baseball images.

So, try the odd batter grip of Ty Cobb's? Recontext, minimize, reframe the hold, the swing.

Then bust it out.

He valiantly decided to give that sliver-of-sweet- part of-Mary a break. Create for her a fun lesson. Deliver a prepared slightly mystical pitch, a fun curve ball. After the next meal. She would be asked to sit and please listen to what he was planning for his next semester's introductory speech! And so....

In the morning, he motioned to the more comfortable make-shift seat, and began:

"Hello Dear Ladies and Gentlemen!" and ONLY looked at HER face as though *she was his most well liked, main student,* "Welcome, Class! YOU are one of FOUR classes, already over-filled! Excellent professors draw in LARGE amounts of students! My focus is ONLY on YOU, deeply! He didn't lose contact with Mary's eyes. WE are ready to conduct a one-on-one in case we're stuck together after a very sad wreck somewhere! ALL about YOU, just YOU!"

Then he grinned.

"And I won't attribute any 'narci' word labels, either. No personal validation processing!"

. Holy cow, she already knew that remembering all students was not in their contracts! *Her* issue.

She smiled. And all was good between them that entire day. But not perfect, as he ached with homesickness for his ivory tower pitching mounds in front of an eager-faced class.

115

Yellow Pad Found December 21, 2020.

Professor Merrick. p/21 of 52 (8/20/20)

There's no visibly defined boundary between invisible sounds and barely visible lights. No skin, no shell. Dusky sunlight and moonlight and my own flashlight barely help. My own human sight is inferior to others of the animal kingdom (as is also hearing, smell, taste). Very unlike an owl's or a whale's. About vibration and matter: I remind myself all the time: energy = matter.

Again noted, nothing can be scientifically tested and then published without support and a peer-reviewed process. Regarding what's been witnessed, all the phenomena, I'd love to have understood enough by now to formulate a hypothesis. But better, be able to hold my pets. That would certainly help.

August 21, 2020, Veterinarian in the College City

A blonde lady, in her late twenties, disembarks from an old but newly painted blue station wagon. She'd parked in the veterinarian's lot. She looks at the windows to straighten her hair. Gracefully she removes a secondhand pet carrier from the back seat. Its plastic sharp edges hit and then scrape her knees.

Hours before she was called in by the vet about Michael Merrick's pets. She was the only urgency contact listed by Mike.

Inside, the veterinarian repeated that his staff had tried calling Mike, but his voice mailbox was full. He'd even tried contacting the university. Mike was to return after the holidays.

116

The administration hadn't acknowledged him missing, since, of course, it was okay to be absent - while taking his sabbatical.

The dog's slumping, whining and lack of sleep was disheartening. He had been biting himself, agitated. Mike's bird and cat lost appetites. So, she, Lucille, carried some special healthy treats and a pet health book.

After an hour with the dog, she suggested playing music in a private room. Using a birdfeeder with water, she asked the doctor permission to add sugar. After music filled the room, using her cell phone, she petted and hummed, then finger-fed, and throughout the hours talked softly to each of them.

The vet silently gazed at her coddling the pets, and it seemed to work magically. Then as she dialed Mike's cell, turned up the volume, and allowed Mike's outgoing announcement message voice to fill the room, he couldn't believe his eyes.

She repeated this three times.

When seeing ears perk up, Lucille was convinced they recognized his voice and be feeling better, soon. The wagging and the purring and the singing bird showed - much better.

Yellow Pad Found December 21, 2020.
Professor Merrick. p/ 25 of 52 (8/22/20)

Nuances in diction, timbre, vibration, speed, volume and other homo sapient concepts keep my focus. (Vocalization characteristics) and its sound is recorded on my cell. Still can't categorize. All this magnifies maybe a fact there's an intended meaning from energy in the cave which can intuitively mimic yet ineffectively transmit meaning. Ah, I assume it intends to transmit meaning. See the study dilemma here? Our world is beautiful, I must say now, so not totally go insane. I am utilizing elocution, as do bats, I try locating areas nearest the cave entry to locate where walls begin to turn. Trying to figure out how the sound is so different.

Odd structures? Odd instruments' original shapes?

LUMINSTRATUM

Grey, unclear Skies behind David Anthony and My Lady

David Anthony: Yes, odd shapes. Structure of the instruments bring distinct music. The odd elements in them are caused by reactions in outer space. Particles land, form, break, They then reform as unclassified, are rare or odd – they use miniscule particles of metal of odd electron configurations.

My Lady: Okay, TMI right now! The question from Dr. Merrick isn't what happens in outer space. His question is why the sound is happening there, it is an unheard of sound. And he can't see from where it originates.

David Anthony: There is fusion. It caused our sun and earth to exist, and there's fission for the splitting of a heavy atom into smaller pieces. Fusion is the joining of light atoms into a heavy one. Both processes convert a tiny amount of matter into large amounts of energy. They work in opposite directions and have very different requirements, fuels, and consequences.

My Lady: You studied and learned more than I care to ever know. I don't remember even wanting to understand science I might not make it as far in this ministry for that.

But you still are missing the dilemma, here, David Anthony.
Why is its origin and location a big unseen mystery?

David Anthony: *Every spirit has its essentiality. And every being must be finely tuned to become self-mastered.*

My Lady: *And there is an answer. Truth. It shouldn't point to always being a test of belief or faith. That is what the cruelty of religion is, telling people to just swallow it all.*

WVC August 24

"Know about sperm whales?" Mike asks, his feet drag on the dirt, interrupting breakfast chat. Nobody's smiling?"

They sit stone-faced this morning and swallow fish sprinkled with wheat germ and marinated in soy sauce. Again. Last night fish smothered by a can of mushroom soup. Before that, tomato ketchup and croutons.

"A sperm whale's vocalization, for instance, has been studied by oceanographers, audiologists and other scientists for decades. Maybe others with finer specializations have also! These whales communicate something: So, 150 repeatable patterns known as 'codas' belonging to the sperm whale?"

"Really?" both Jude and Janna are truly captivated.

"Their broadband clicks place sound ranges above a human's hearing capacity – all sound comes from a whale's nasal passage. Experts say their language is complex, nuanced. Nuances like these exist in all the kingdom's creatures."

All three of them look straight at each other and smile.

"Wow!" Jude laughs. He left the fish sitting uneaten. Now

lying on his back, his feet push football sized rocks in the fire pit. This has become his daily work out.

Mary quips, "oh, so you are whale watching at night?"

"Sperm whales? Moby Dick was a sperm whale, a white one, Melville's symbol of the universe." Jude quips again.

"We're mighty lucky for a cerebrum, cerebellum and a thumb. Otherwise, we likely wouldn't have ever created a darn thing. Nor had a van or copter to crash." Mary spouts.

The new WVC's second plastic container contraption catches his eye, a lounging chair! Cushioning airbags! He and Jude started creating them two days ago. By flashlight. Mike slumps right into it, he didn't sleep any hours while waiting for sounds last night on the grassy knolls.

While supine and fading, he recalls tiny lights he'd spotted when 'fully awake' at the cave. Now he relaxes more.

REMs, now dreaming. There he is at junior high school.

Miniscule, yet chunkier heaps of unidentified metals are scattered on the class floor, reflecting a waning moonlight - in color. Now dreaming deeper, he's a teen, sitting at his high school desk, talking metallics. No attention from anyone.

Jotting creatively, he adds sound attributes to floating orbs, he notes their evolvement, attributes character names, cultural histories, spiritual, karmic agendas. It's like his periodic social psychology table. He titles each one a music piece. He begins to design a play and a dialogue.

Each orb, he tells the continuingly inattentive classmates, encloses a soul. He begins singing. His pencil works faster. The instructor flashes angry eyes and thrusts the syllabus to hit Mike's cheek. He tries. He can't propel his breath to shout back.

Stunned awake he sees Janna's brown eyes looking straight at him, only inches away. "Mike, calm down!"

Janna says, "Mike? You were singing, your hands were writing in the air! Then you yelled, "you don't know what you're talking about!' So loud! It was so funny! You yelled they were sheep, faking belief. You said – and it was so funny – that they were parroting, they knew nothing, were afraid to admit it!"

Mary nods, concurs, "Janna described it, yes, spewing saliva, too! Who was in that dream? My goodness!" she giggles softly, looks in his eyes. "Your face was like one of the avatars Jude drew yesterday!"

Mike hadn't intentionally said 'crbs,' loathing possibilities of being viewed as a paranormal weirdo.

Chapter FIVE

Yellow Pad Found December 21, 2020.
Professor Merrick. p/27 of 52 (8/23/20)

In the past two weeks, I've alluded how cultures throughout the world attribute meaning in symbolic form, well, here goes again!

Rarely in any culture can two people exactly understand what is being said, back and forth. Language is inadequate. Something is always amiss while sending words and receiving, in quality or quantity, such as sound, meaning, intent, correct definition, tense, structure, context, receptivity. Often in our fast-paced society, a need for a concept or thing needs correct words. The list is grand for ones which

need to make headway through consensus.
Establishing connection with another
person's cognitive framework or emotional
state needs well-developed vocabularies and
experiential comprehensive understandings
of individuals. The capacity to visualize
concepts enhances clarity in communication.

He assesses then enters the WVC quietly. They're all up, drinking camp coffee or canned coke. He empties a bag full of soil and large glittery metallic chunks. Showing irritation, Mary scoots her plate of food to avoid dust and tiny particles.

"Does anyone know what these particles are?" Janna and Mary hobble away, uninterested. Jude mutters, "evidence of an archeological dig? Prehistoric artists forgot to neaten up their supplies? Can I have it to make clay?"

"When new minerals are found, like from a meteorite, elements in atom classification are important. 'New' means its chemical make-up differs from others already recorded. They're new to science."

"You found that stuff near where, now?"

"Near the cave's ground - hill gives off sounds and lights." His stomach knots, sinks. Uh, whoops, his secret. Zip it -- fast.

"Oooh! sounds from a cave? Tell us more!"

Petrified. He isn't ready.

He diverts, backtracks. "These are products of fusion power within stars. They spew across the cosmos on the blast waves of supernovae. They mix with raw ingredients. They are likely from other planets, too. The universe, which is matter and energy, includes galaxies. And there are billions of galaxies."

"But the cave stuff? You want to talk?"

He still ignores, "Likely, countless universes beyond ours. An estimated septillion stars, many with a nearby rocky-metallic planet, my campers, is noticed from all parts of the universe – our galaxy! The Milky Way is always seen. There are more galaxies. Sometimes the galaxies collide."

Mary adds from her new chair, "Some asteroids have valuable metals. Like the Psyche one, is it Psyche 6?"

"So, psyche and metals today! No checking on our behavior? Why aren't you letting us hear about some psychedelic cave happening? Comparing glittery new rocks?" Janna smiles genuinely. Then she coughs. Then she sneezes.

"Cover your mouth!" Mary yells.

"Psychos," Jude inserts.

Mike taps Mary's shoulder lightly, then signals with his index finger for her to follow. He heads to the plastic tub furniture by the wrecked van. Looking into her eyes, "Mary, I have reams of paper stored inside. I will help you assemble more Squib books."

"What? Why?"

"'Your face shows a happier person whenever you are writing down your thoughts; you've already filled the one you packed. And others here also need something like this to do."

Her face shows endeared anxiety.

Mike noted her alarm, "Mary, I have only scanned over a few pages of your writing," He fibs. He'd been more curious than reading just a few of the pages.

"Mike, I'm surprised you took any interest!"

123

LUMINSTRATUM

Blue Clear Skies behind David Anthony and My Lady.

My Lady: Splitting of a heavy atomic nucleus, is that
        correct, Dave Anthony?

David Anthony: Yes! You are learning!

My Lady: From cosmic dust, an astronaut, solar wind,
        and many other ways. A meteorite seems to have hit that
        camp, long ago! Also maybe when those campers were at
        that coordinate. We will ask about that.

My Lady: The answer, please, of from where the sound
        is originating, who or what is playing it. That is the
        perplexment of Dr. Merrick. We've leapt back and forth to
        "faith and belief" seen them speak of soul and spirit. Merrick
        understands essence, you know ontological, but he
        desperately is seeking a teleological explanation. Yes, the
        answers are there, and they remain invisible gifts from the
        Supreme" but we are seeing how it has been skipped over,
        unexplained satisfactorily. Almighty is not fully disclosing
        what we ask for.

David Anthony: Why are we employed in much literature to
        relay what is privy for humans to know for certain -- or not.
        As though hiding parts of truth to bait with a carrot while
        professing that we love and car by carrying God's love for
        them, being hostage ourselves awaiting the almighty
        command for perpetuating love.

My Lady: We need to find out from the Supreme about the
        true reasons why religion presents us with verses and games.
        It has to do with allowance and receptivity. Explain, God,
        please, how! In a teleological manner, not purely ontological
        faith works in all of this.

David Anthony: Hmmm, need I go into lip tension and the sound of your instrument? Contributes to the pitch and depth of all clarity. Think this... Same Note, Different Instrument.

My Lady: Oh, careful. Lips and tension bring memories of me being matter and am now focusing on stuff I can't partake while only a spirit. Am I being harassed by an angel?

More instructions with a higher agenda are arriving soon. We will be closer when more is investigated or shared by others. Oh, look! All the metallic pieces on the ground, shining so vibrantly. Even if mere messengers, we too are limited. We don't know or might never learn all answers.

Moments later, sitting on chairs shaded by a tree, the two use two stumps as tables. Seven Squib Books are assembled and blank sheets are stapled, ready. She marks her name on each one. Each will hold a week's worth of her thoughts.

Looking at his face closely she feels him. She smiles, he looks happy, his skin glows. They work quickly and well.

"Wish I could be back home before these are filled."

"Mary, keep in mind the books you said your daughter helped with. I will make more to give to other campers."

Yards away, munching on jerky, Jude spies them talking, their heads close. He notes body language. Are they intimate? Beyond simply caring? Odd lights catch his eyes, floating above their heads, disappearing then reappearing, floating.

Jude blinks. The circular areas move fast but boundaries are not definite, they're elliptic overlaps.

He blinks, rubs his eyes. Without touching, Mary and Mike continue seeing only each other, and both rub and knead when pain bothers. Self-massages are habitual now.

Jude continues scrutinizing, tightening his face. The bright sun narrows his gaze, he crosses his brows, he knows his eyes squint but does not want to miss a thing between the two, especially whatever it is above their heads.

Mike limps back to the WVC firepit. Mary catches Jude's expression: he stares hard at her face. It unnerves her because his gaze is eerie, triggering prior memories during the first two days. He'd darted his sneery glances at her. She feels victimized even though the'd been making headway on a trusting friendship. She'd tried to keep her Squib book from everyone.

She stalls, her legs ache. Slowly she reaches her big rock beside her Squib Book and paper stacks. Restudy? The already completed 'Week 8/3/20 at WVC' Squib Booklet faces her, as though placed there. In that one she'd written about Jude's eerie tare scrutinizing her that first night. It might soon be time to share this with Jude. Maybe others will know Squibbing.

'It's midnight, almost August 3rd. Their flatulence wafts from their sleeping bag to my nostrils and it makes me sick. Politely asking them what they ate can't work and are filled with disgust and anger about our being strewn and stranded here and now with them. Everyone is a physical and emotional ball of pain. Instead, I'd whispered loudly that they both stank.'

That night, she continued writing, arrogantly so, contrasting economic and educational status prior to knowing them at all. *'Also, that photo of a blond girl sitting next to Mike unnerves me. I am irked by the Junipers' stench. Suddenly a southern physical urgency is beckoning. I grab my purse. I check my wallet contents, not trusting their looks, having categorized them as petty thefts. When jerking to check, it hurts., I yelp with each limping step! I head to my business bush.*

Jude was snickering the entire time, and I hated him for it.'

She'd continued that first night, toward the business bush, to shroud herself while crouching. No tissue paper existed.

126

She'd frantically searched her purse for anything that might wipe. Was relieved and thankful for a crumpled paper receipt.

Starting to stand, her foot slid on her business. While walking out from the bush, she'd noted too late her shoe was carrying a chunk of it. "Oh, No! YUCK!" she'd hollered.

As Jude watched that dusk, he'd picked up on it all - as he seemed often to be doing - then offered another sneer, like what they'd both been exchanging.

He'd then said, she'd written, '*Hey, Mary…Mary Hawkings, a college person. You could kill the stench with spray cologne. Pick wildflowers to decorate your hole! Show everyone here you're above it, you are, aren't you? I mean, are you really that new to dumps in the woods? The privileged always keep up quite the most decorated hole! Smile, accept, make happy out of this!' Lose the negs, lady. Wow, like an animal you will carry your bottom smell. The stink of it. Wanna get high now? Mary?*'

He'd then succeeded in shaming her, and she felt anger, hate. She'd continued to feel it toward him, for days.

Mary stops reading, looks up and decides it is time to level up with Jude about a lot of things. She catches his eyes. "Jude," she says to him, sweetly, "I want you to read this and comment to me what is going on. Sometime. You should know now exactly how I perceived you a few weeks ago."

Like Mike's summoning of baseball heroes, after she loans the Squib book to Jude, she recalls a memory -- about Meg. This is her current saving grace now, visualizing Meg. Years ago, together, they'd painted Squib book covers with pasted letters spelling out: "Mother Squibbler, Mary's Bagger-of-It-All"

Still wondering what's 'sounding out'. I'll call it hum-singing. Is it of a bird? A primate? Mountain lions can chirp, right?

When I nodded off on a grassy knoll last night, five distinctly separate voices sang words about houses. Yes, houses. I recognized the word 'houses' in Spanish, too. Leaving dying houses which are no longer suitable for a human soul. Words in other languages seemed to describe a shell covering, a cloak. Then – some call this synchronicity - when returning to the campsite, houses as shields until death was the topic! Synchronicity is becoming quite prevalent here. I am sane and highly amused with faith.

WVC August 26th, a.m.

Check! All feathers are in their pristine surrealness. He imagines being carried by those wings to fly far from here.

By 9:00 a.m. he reenters the WVC. The ambiance is level; their faces look solemn. Alcohol has long gone depleted, so it's clearheaded chimera. He listens. Houses. Each soul is inside a house. Each consciousness is a soul. Bodies are houses carrying souls from place to place. Nothing makes complete logical sense to him, it's poetry, it's art, but here that's the new normal.

It is difficult for Mike. He admits his entitled attitude is warranting snippy dismissiveness over the new age woo woo flow. Janna mentions that when someone dies, it is only the house dying. He is beginning to appreciate her filtering. Her sleepy slurring has stopped sans pain killers.

"Well!" Janna stumbles. "Old wounds inside my house

128

have needed healing, I am-obsessed about outward decoration. Mary opened that can of worms the first day here!"

"Armor grew. My 'beauty' armor attracted, then outrageously warded off weaker predators. I was saying 'look at me' but beware! Doesn't mean you can have me, just beware!'"

"You said you're done with lashes and make up."

"Packed no eyelashes. I seem naked Make-up adds a sense of false confidence."

"Have to admit hypocrisy, yes! I put make-up on ladies to earn money! Untrained for much else. Someday I can focus on nutrients for the nails, hair, and skin.

At that second, Mary shouts, "Ugh, what is this, the pattern, it looks like plastic or something….!'"

The others hobble over to where she is looking, on the rock she sits on when reading or writing. She is pointing to a dried snakeskin that was recently shed. They all take 15 minutes to search where a snake would be recovering, three people at once poking and moving possible hiding places.

Later, at dinner, chatter resumes about warrior shields and appearances. It was a suitable time for a short lesson.

"Since ancient times, genders instinctively competed for mates. Many subcultures exist today, and scientists actively study them." Mike looked around. All were listening.

"More modern civilizations now consider what is brought to the marital table beyond outer looks and childrearing ability or domestication skills. The deeper the education, the more careful they are in partnering and family planning."

129

He continues, "Loads of assorted variables here! Much depends on cultural indoctrination! Wide noses and pointy huge teeth have their beauty somewhere else within various cultures."

Mary asked, "Janna, do you know yourself better?"

"I'm conscious I no longer will conform to standards that I didn't create unless I've thought it through. Others cultivated an 'acceptable standard,'" Janna began, "Others' sculpting others for different reasons."

"Many communities greatly value their libraries. I hear you talk and see how naturally curious you are. Look at Greek Mythology! The Goddess Psyche was revered in her beauty. Psyche is also the Goddess of Soul. Dang! We can't research this today, no online searches." Mary offered.

Jude asks, "Their 'souls'? Or their habits? I won't fake understanding any of this!"

"Delving there, buddy! I am trying to be a listener today here. No theologist could help us?" Mike smiles. "Individuals transform while in new group situations."

"Hey guys. My body has felt like crap since being here. I didn't choose this. Some crappy fatalist would say it did. Our suffering needs fixing. Again, not pretending to swallow this," Jude offers, throwing everyone into a careful pause.

Being quiet was good. Enough. All felt the soft wind moving through pines, all heard the flapping wings of birds, smelled smoke from the fire. Watching steam fold, lump, then stretch gracefully from the water pot was topped by the scurrying squirrels and chatter of the chipmunks.

Jude continues, "I don't think our forever lasting souls, as they say, last. The brain is gone when we die, the heart has stopped. Leaving room for hope, though."

"We're poets when we don't have answers," Janna smiled.

Mike adds, "Ever visit affluent areas? Gorgeous houses?! People with money define what everyone's happiness ought to be. A symbolic object. Then more money will go into selling it -- for more. More is never enough. The cycle repeats."

"Are habitats improving their communication?" Mary grins.

"Maybe sometimes! Disconnections will occur, only for a bit." Mike looks straight into Mary's eyes, hers dart off, then she checks back to allow his softness to enter in.

A deer hawk swoops in, startling all. It lands on a little mouse, hooks onto it, in a split-second launch to fly from the dinner crumbs. All of them sit in awe of the suddenness, how three seconds changed the feel of the entire evening.

Yellow and orange flames thrown from logs provide the only light. Janna, in ultra-quiet mode is clutching her abdominal area. She struggles to inhale., squints rubbing her coronal plane.

Mary and Mike edge carefully nearer to her. Jude is nervous, unable to speak. His guts and hands shake.

The weight in her sadness needs letting out. It does. For twenty minutes, between sobs, she spews incidents of abuse by family members. Everything began at age ten. In rapid, broken sentences, she chunks incidences. Pregnant at thirteen and after. Alter outward appearance to control her world more.

She was forced to give up her twins by the father when they were a few months old. She began a multiple foster parent alteration, a cycle, back and forth, not to see them. Her sobbing is loud and deep, and her groaning diaphragm pains the others.

One family finally adopted them. This was news to Jude. Unknowing the full reason why Janna gave her children up for adoption. This secret had been held for years, while married.

His face changes, he moves in closer, then asks if he can touch her. He lightly massages her knees. Tears track down her dusty cheeks. She looks at all, smiles.

Reaching out to him and to the others for hugs, he kisses her forehead, her cheeks, her hands.

"I obtusely went bold - cosmetically! I got skilled! I was proud to tell women clients how to apply makeup. How to look sexier. I was paid. Only thing I could do well for money. Their need was mostly meant to attract, allure, compete."

Cognitive dissonance, Mike concludes, privately. Sorry but glad about Janna appearing to be arriving at a junction. Her process to find inner truth and entrusting witness was key.

The WVC site's collective conscious energy had been gifted. Lifted. Each camper slowly turned to touch offer gentle hugs, then they repeated while avoiding more physical pain.

Driving from Gardenia View- August 27th

It was unusually foggy for late August. Rudy noted it wasn't humid. This lowered his mood. Even more than the last hour's heart sinking visit. Now, absorbing that the only woman he'd ever loved, all her wonderful attributes, made his heart soft. In front of his eyes, she was fading.

He decided he should increase the number of phone calls with her but without all the medical staff noise around them. He should arrange more cyber meetings with increased clarity and without bedside staff wearing muffling masks.

His most successful associates knew what was happening and why but rarely spoke up about how careless all the politicians were. They saw daily how specialized media material attracted and supported a demographic audience, more for planned manipulation. All arguments had their own flaws.

Half an hour ago he'd overheard a nursing home hallway conversation. While sitting beside Dena's bed, rolling gurneys and shushed voices got his attention. Abruptly there was a cover up of the fact that seventeen patients and staff had moved suddenly to another section without an issued statement of reason. The virus was a stigma; the medical field knew it. A sign was posted: ***Change masks every 30 minutes.***

The meat of his current depression dawned. It was seeded when Liam and Ned, who'd planned to accompany him, had canceled without stating a reason. Both promised they'd call their mother soon. Annella didn't give even a lame excuse. Rudy considered they'd all likely speak with a professional about it. That's what Dena would want, anyway.

The common thread he saw, was that the new emotions needed navigation. He dictated: "Dashboard Calendar! Confer with counselors skilled in child rearing. Flag! Remind daily."

The doctors remarked how she'd been receiving the latest, yet nobody noticed improvements. Staff did mention how Dena's spirits rose whenever Shawna was by her side.

The dock was forty minutes away. What now? Free to wallow?. Never a pill taker, a drinker or a smoker. Moods didn't change without Dena's nearby help. Once at a formal dinner he was placed to sit near an astrologer who professed expertise in emotions and planetary orbits. Rudy laughed when told his moon and mutable sun sign meant he was "overly" sensitive.

People accepted nonsense readily. Gullibility will help the crooked sales personnel. The richest have this practice down.

Should he have his assistant call Rhetta to affirm logistics? Scheduled for November, yes, checked! Calendar green flagged, meaning Dena finished due diligence profiling weeks ago. Today Dena informed Rudy their investigator, Don Creed, gathered Rhetta's research info to make sure about Rhetta.

One of Don's reports mentioned he'd learned how Rhetta behaved after a librarian shared some personal details with her. Her mother's unaffordable nursing home had caused the librarian and her husband to take on extra jobs to pay for it. Even Rudy, when reading Don's report, couldn't believe the hefty monthly price. It costs more than a monthlong high-end cruise would. Other reports showed Rhetta receiving many case studies on philanthropic donations – worldwide.

How had Don captured all of this?

Fine skills, that sly guy Don Creed had, always utilizing a magic vacuum for information. He could draw blood from boulders. There were 61 files already. Rhetta girl had been busy! Rudy often wondered what tactics Don used. He was good, always had been for the Marchers. Lied easily, second nature.

Rudy didn't like lies. Dissonance stirred him. Dena's current thumbs up. Likely, she'd seen several investigative reports, scrutinizing Rhetta's motivation as well as various commitments. No red flags about Rhetta's public reputation.

"Remember this quote, always, Fawn," Dena had said, reminding him of T.S. Eliot. "The most trouble in this world is caused by people wanting to be important."

In the early days of building their business and family, he and Dena were deceived by con artists who skillfully won over the Marchers' trust and avoided responsibility. The Marchers vowed it would not happen again. Money attracted the best of the worst. A few more of them entered the game, though, and quickly, cunningly assessed how to lie their heads off.

The Marcher's almost three times lost a ton of money, but thankfully, in time, they put their heads together to figure out all the logic and math, and began to deeply listen, to detect. They became astutely aware of the red flag warnings.

About Rhetta, the only red flags were years without committed boyfriends or besties, or jobs she'd stayed with longer than three years (she was still young and searching). Her grades through college were top notch perfect, though.

"We've already run through a couple of tests for potential trouble. She's clear. More probes by November will filter even more. Give me a week or so to plan." Rudy had said.

Dena ordered that, in the meantime, hire financial investigators to obtain details on each child's assets, spending, plans to sell anything. What had they shared with friends? The reports were to reach Dena by the end of the month.

But again, he figured Dena was on top of it – especially in terms of fiscals, even when having acute pain and still declining pain meds. Staff knew she sought clarity and closure. She preached that the kids' actions defined family legacies. But, Rudy pleaded, remember them as kids.

Sure. Get to their truly innocent years. One night both joked about the nature of each child. While they were very raw and young. Remember comical activities while the kids were little and inspired to imagine. They were to describe how fictional cities could be like. Later, how they'd create them.

First, they learned to read maps, then to draw road signs. Liam designed a city where everything related to candy, and Dena would laugh at his ingenious billboard art, '*Cotton Candy is Just Dandy,*' and the homes all had candy corn shaped chimneys and bright tinted minty glass.

Of course, when returning home from a convention or conference, there would be something a sitter hadn't noticed.

135

Liam once painted the upstairs windows a licorice black.

Once Annella dyed the hair on every doll, using food coloring (her city was for women's beauty), and Ned took chicken and steak bones out of the trash to bury in the backyard. (His was a city for health with hospitals, churches, and the cemetery.)

How and what would they acquire after naming all their needs? This is what Rudy and Dena instilled. Plan, plan what could be next. Assess, figure it out! The two happily watched their children transform and soon were capable to meet their objective. They already had all they needed. Everything easily.

Insight was gained on how to set up activities with adults. The Marcher's party guests included candidates hoping for jobs, then be encouraged to plot that 'city game'...Your 'favorite scenario project?' during appetizers. Insightfulness. Eventually each interviewed candidate would 'describe an ideal community,' and think honestly after being asked 'how you'd accomplish every single result you just stated you wanted?'

Candidates liked to play, plan and dream. The Marcher's belief was that one should be put on the spot. An aim was to plan how to gain, how to win, or how to please Rudy and Dena with 'the' correct business project plan. They could create one themselves, revealing true selves. If totally in charge of every decision affecting outcomes, the Marchers took notes, assessed each one's caliber and skilled leadership.

How to overcome then transform problems into opportunities? Rudy trailed slightly, still behind Dena about the importance of a legacy was. But as their circles grew, he grew.

He continued reminiscing, driving. The fog cleared as the popping dashboard messages prompted him with reminders to gather details, to ensure new building developments. Commuter airport constructions, quotas status and timelines. While the sun suddenly threw a beautiful hue through his window, and a pair of white doves flew near, he smiled and felt calmness, easing the conversations about the delays of several small planes he'd bought, and when confirming dates for investors to gather logistics – schedule yacht meetings, close on sales.

AUGUST 29TH, Home of Gracie

Meghan thumbed the blue notebook sharing her research responses to Theresa Land after minutes of them both boxing more items to carry out. Reponses were well thought out and stoic, Mrs. Land assessed, minute-by-minute she'd studied how Meghan's emotions varied each day. After the first week of Mary's missing status, essential staples of Meghan's items were transported to the Land's. Today Meghan pointed to various new items to transport, items like a camera, an old tape recorder, a pair of her mom's earrings and more photos. It had been four weeks. Nothing about Mary arrived them.

Meghan pointed to the wall photo of a man who, by now, she believed could be her father. With wide, saddened eyes, she asked Mrs. Land questions about it. Mrs. Land had no answers. "I think Dave is his name and that they never married. I don't know much, Sweetie."

"'Just write every night, using a new thought, and research it' are words Momma had told me right before I went to camp. I will keep doing it until she returns." Meghan swallowed then teared. Both were holding on to fear and to hope.

This would be their third search through Mary's desk and other drawers. Today the dean called Mrs. Land to ask where Mary's aunt Madeline lived. The college's IT had spotted her name in Mary's email queue. An upcoming family reunion?

Mary's address book listed Madeline Hawkings, but a phone number had been penciled out. The dean said his assistant would try the aunt's email for a response.

Mary hadn't mentioned the trip to Theresa or to Gracie, and for two weeks after moving Meghan all three had knocked on every close by neighbors' doors, asking questions and providing missing flyers to pass around. Mary kept herself private, and quiet – this, the neighbor's consensus.

The task *Beliefs about a Deity and/or Creator* rested beside Mary's home computer. Meghan wanted to focus more on her mom's assignment and took her mom's task book. Today she added in it an assignment, her own words, the one soaking her interest. It was '*mother*' and '*father*'.

She asked Mrs. Land if she could take photos to the guest room where her other items were. Was it okay with Mrs. Land? Yes. Then, Meghan asked, "Please let me take that large hanging portrait off this wall, it's my dad. I want to hang it."

Again, emotion stirred Theresa often to ask for help from Gracie whose first college semester was trying. The last phone call brought unfamiliar tension in Gracie's voice. "Just, please, honey, connect with Meggie a few times more each week, she's having a rough time -- we both miss you!"

Every day, they'd call Mary, every day the voice mail was full. They filed a missing status report. Detectives would revisit.

That evening Meghan checked the old recorder, both it and a flashlight needed batteries Under the bedsheets., seconds after pushing 'play' and using earplugs, she heard her mom's voice and a man's. They conversed about studying chemistry; intimate one minute, and harsh the next. the man usually softly called her, 'Dear Mary.' She called himme 'Sweet Davie'.

WVC Noon, Hill Base

"The Detouristing Cave entities wait for me," he joked juvenilely to himself. Mike was greeted. Literally. For ten seconds. They started up, on cue, as though they had watched him arrive. His favorite soothing music played! Lights! Too many days without him! He found his softest knoll with the coolest grass.

Hey buddy, examine this! Leaning toward arrogance? Yes, I feel important enough. No, not a narcissist, I don't need psychological counseling.

Yellow Pad Found December 21, 2020.
Professor Merrick. p/32 of 52 8/29/20)

(Do afterlives require one to direct traffic?)

Words of music last night moved rhythmically. They talked of afterlife during a brand-new tempo. The lights, orbs or photons danced, too!

I noticed five different colored owls on trees surrounding the opening of the cave, all on their own branches, very still, sitting above me. The dusk passed, the owls stayed perched, their eyes seemed to never shut. Superior vision. They represent 'culture', symbol of wisdom and stillness.

Countries have many subcultures. I repeatedly write this. Holidays, relationships, behavioral cues, each different wherever one travels.

I have not followed closely with any deity defined by my own culture here in the USA. I see no reason to be identified as a member of a religious system. I could be a Pantheist, as forced religion has disconnected me. Don't even identify with a subculture.

Heaven and hell are terms indicating polarizing realms of bliss or torture. All enforce using fear-induced dogma. It insinuates 'getting there' is based on behavior. The 'quality' of 'after life' implies a deity is determining spiritual future. Social psychologist colleagues agree healthier afterlife beliefs and faiths are largely intuitive rather than taught or learned. I am thankful for that.

Mary reopened her first weeks of Squib Book to check titles of the abstracts Mike then had loaned her. She'd read all of them. She ventured again: *Mike left for wherever he goes at night, but I asked him to dig his stacks for me. Minutes later he emerged from the WV to hand me 'Idealism in Diversity,' 'Theories About Souls' Social Impacts of Mass Disasters,' 'Belief and Faith in 1600's' Schizophrenia Findings 1950-2010,' 'Narcissism in Parenting' and 'Boundaries within Non-Secularity.'*

I am wondering what the heck was he planning to utilize from these studies during that sabbatical. I had already asked but he remained vague.

When he was handing them to me, he was smiling. All he mentioned was, "These are oldie but goodie studies," then pointed to the dozing Junipers, and yelled, "Hey! Wake up all! Regular interaction between members of different groups reduces prejudice, but only under favorable conditions! Our conditions are not favorable, and we all know it. So, DO attempt to create one! Bodies sitting in pain and not trying means you've resigned to simply be

140

losing than gaining!'

Mary swallowed her tears. Each camper's physical functioning hadn't measurably changed much. Each had gotten used to it, pained and crumpled as in the first days here. At least all had sought healing inside their hearts. All were sharing, getting along much better.

Yellow Pad Found December 21, 2020.

Professor Merrick. p/35 of (9/??)

How could entities read another's mind? I use instinct and avoid claiming anything else.

Some say one can't effectively measure or test emotions -- Attempts to scientifically test rarely show consistent data.

Question Everything. That has been my motto.

What are called 'orbs' (a co-camper mentioned he knew a bit about orbs, yet I am always careful to request qualifiable resources!) I never would believe what they were weeks ago and still have a hard time.

Supernaturalism and spiritualism – I've not the slightest study in. Also, we question meanings of souls, lately. Some believe that souls aren't something bodies possess, instead, they argue that our souls are what actually have bodies.

I continue to keep this private, being perplexed as a professor, I am to deliver empirical back up.

I'd be an idiot professor trying to teach feebly, as lately this is true, I have been. But I feel beautiful, loving forces beyond my personal understanding.

On some days, Rhetta would be enthralled whenever reading philanthropic success stories. But she remained uncertain.

Fighting strife, a consultant told her to focus on moving forward, using natural curiosities. Feel her heart. "Seek, Rhetta, check populaces, discover ways to find how communities collectively think. The median, the average. What binds them, how they express. See why and how, and which media, what they buy."

Always use exact research data. Don't fudge or impose your opinion or will with charts or spreadsheets! Never manipulate facts or figures. Gain trust. Know your stuff. Heartening will fuel and propel compassion. Set rigid budgets toward a grand goal.

Weigh a philanthrope's concern. They'll sense it and gradually be wearing your shoes with both you and them inside of them, especially when shooting for the moon. Know the visceral depths of potential support when asking for proper funding.

Remember, billionaires know billionaires. And influencers must - if they want to be effective – strongly feel to grasp issues.

Something else was energized around her. Like being under surveillance. A logical possibility was the Marchers had investigators probing her activities. Something she would never share with anyone, understanding herself to be tad paranoid.

The monied always stayed ahead of each game. She understood they were versed in implementing plans, as axioms set for centuries had fail-proof stats, dedication, drives. Don't attend just with an open palm. Have a dedicated passion.

Ready, get set, Rhetta Dear. Oh, but...

Today's hurdle was a broken air conditioning system. It was 103 degrees today. She grabbed an icy beer.

She phoned her cousin who lived five miles away. They agreed to meet. Indian summer weather, why not? Her cousin worked for a private foundation and Rhetta had her list of questions ready. Together they'd approach people, lightly chat, laugh, survey strangers' thoughts on issues then gather opinions and collect data from varieties of targeted social strata. Together she and her cousin had a wonderful afternoon with people.

Don't fear being brutally honest. Rhetta shared with her cousin how senior librarians were now probing about her motivation, sharing how she'd crafted a new response to that, smiling kindly: "I am a bit surprised you asked! Why is it considered? How is it concerning? You found resources, right?"

Her cousin laughed when she shared narcissist types - communal narcissism studies and articles were trending. Hoping never to emulate those models, Rhetta decided to question what she was doing and why. How to help others develop a better life, a greater change affecting many.

Today she would drink, then forgive herself for being human. She recorded all her thoughts ranging from the grandiose to the lame. Let it flow, she'd edit and refine later.

Three hours after her cousin went home, she reviewed their fun. How they'd spent hours in the hot sun canvassing and questioning, laughing, and taking notes. She was bushed. Yes, pillow. A pillow with another beer. She wished for party favors. She fell asleep smiling, watching baseball game.

She dreamt she had walked in a newly forming town and was interviewing how the United States outshone all the other developed countries.

Some began shouting about immigration, others about clean, renewable energy, homelessness, cost of education, health care, climate change and the elderly. Her list started trailing behind her like a wedding train getting browned by mud.

She awoke feeling exhausted but invigorated. Her favorites had expanded. Again. Smell the coffee.

Later that day, she put down her book and searched for Tyler, her former flame. Use people search, or on social media. After half an hour, she confirmed. His current girlfriend was a lot prettier than she was. And it didn't matter. He likely would mess this relationship up, too.

The next day she visited community centers to assess programs like low-income housing, migrant education and rehabilitation, even childcare, food shelters, and senior help.

She visited nursing homes and compiled data and ideas while carrying humility and heartbreak before returning to her rental.

She swore to remain brutally honest, though, and knew that if she were very rich, she'd lose her now natural inspiration to help fractions of the poor. She noticed that many used to lacking resources seemed complacent. Maybe they'd learned to be helpless due to low energy. She met several pockets showing angry and entitled attitudes.

A richer individual wouldn't have enthusiasm to help unless investable opportunities were there! Not now, but where there's a need, a willful heart, or slightest drive, there's a way.

Yellow Pad Found December 21, 2020.

Professor Merrick. p/39 of 52 (9/20)

Each separate vibration I now safely claim, is
a soul "vocalization," having distinct intensity

144

and pitch. The 'orbs' now rarely appear in my vision. When they arbitrarily do, they don't remain long.

Closely to my ear, a whisper, like, "always been and always will be with you."

This brings me an implication there's been a frequency of "me" not ever noted in my mind until now. As an instructor, I clarify the important role scientists contribute and should avoid holding distorted ideas. Yet, I add that science is not a complete collection of hard final truths. Too many during this pandemic *expressed that they believe science should provide this. Science is a myriad of processes: essence is that it's a never-ending discovery of added learning.*

WVC, September 3, 2020

Tones topics. Walking into the WVC Mike heard Jude describe a soulful glow in his dog's eyes whenever Jude spoke a certain way - with a special tail wag. Mary shared how Meghan absorbed emotions from the womb.

A purring distant motor made their necks arch.

"Planes! Oh, my goodness, please, please fly right over us again, and see us!"

Mary's "amen," was barely audible, her head now in her hands. Seeing all the other eyes were checking her, "all I want to believe is that when I pray, my deity is real. When I don't pray, especially these days, I don't hold hope very well."

Mike steps in, "Humans invented 'reason' and 'logic' conceptuality."

"Weighing quandaries?" Mary laughs. "It's time now to accept all that's happened has its designated purpose."

Jude decides right then, amid Mary's lament to ask Mike if he understood anything about panspermia theory. Some buddies of his, he said, one day brought up over beer, "something about outer space objects like those meteorites you were talking about…."

Mike nodded, "yes, proteins, they float in space. Noted by NASA, been found on comets."

Janna storms. She points to the men, "what does that panspermia theory have to do with what Mary just shared with us? Don't you dudes care what might be going on inside of her?"

The purring distant motors take their focus again, their necks arch to see planes. Mary, Janna and Jude each suck in their breath, watching them fly further away.

Before he prepares for tomorrow's vowed cave visit, he says, "I want to gift a souvenir someday, perhaps?"

The other three, together laugh and say, "to whom?"

But first, starting with Janna! Janna, share your mind, anything you've come to be grateful over, while being stuck here? What's your treasure?"

"Oh, I know what it is." Janna laughed. All were relieved to see her face light up. "I treasure not worrying over eyelashes or fingernail fills! I am free from addiction to drugs."

Jude's turn. "No dealing with neighbors. Wait, guys, you're the neighbors! Next!"

Mary quickly said, "I don't have to remember passwords."

Then Mike fought off tears.

"Tell me. Those four trees that broke on August 2nd? I looked closer yesterday. A big, deep hole was caused by some impact. The bark was scraped, the same scrape on all four trees. What object was penetrating? It must still be deep in the soil now.

Jude mumbled, "sky junk ... broken communication devices... a family of four beavers had gone at it...

Janna, "Right. Then the coyotes pounced and beavers tried to make love on them."

Jude ended with, "... but ate them instead.... then gargantuan white-winged birds flew to attack coyotes by splatting on them."

"Wonder if those planes will ever fly closer to us?" Mike's eyes looked hungry for just that to happen.

Mining more knowledge of asteroids, meteors, and comets filled the campsite with happy chatter, but all were utmost anxious about the planes which had already flown out of sight. They kept looking up at any slightest sound like a dog would, waiting for a master's return.

The next morning, Mike's stomach stirred while preparing to venture alone, deeper into the cave, to dig further. He wanted to build scenarios for the Juniper science lessons.

He started to talk about it.

But Jude and Janna, heads down, were ignoring him. They pointed hard with their index fingers, drumming their own

Squib Books signaling 'no', not open to join him. About anything. Preference of personal privacy. Happy, Mike lets out a sigh.

They'd switched into introverted writers! Mary did this! Even if temporarily, he was glad. They're thinking! Mary already completed her weekly Squib Book – the one the two of them had constructed just days before. Prolific, that's Mary. He smiled.

These camp

ers were fearless and bore it out.

Chapter SIX

Yellow Pad Found December 21, 2020.
Professor Merrick. p/ 42 of 52 (9/?/20)

I didn't question or worry. My courage was strong, walking into the cave at 10 a.m. boldly in, heard nor saw a thing. Nothing. I ventured probably 20 feet into blindness, hesitating to beam up, not wanting to disturb. Nothing was everywhere, as though something had stopped. I touched a wall every few steps. Smooth and cool, only slightly gravelly. Its floor became deeper after several yards into it, I measured my steps. Much metallic shavings were in the soil. The cave's tunnel's width averaged seven steps. It felt like a dorm room. Parts became as large as a 7' by 7' room, and

no theatrics today. Theatrics were absent. I am
hoping all know it wise to stay clear for a while.

More possible variables, independent or dependent, he'd only be guessing. He shook his head. Nothing defined could even qualify as a sample, all fluctuated and changed in there. No theory, no hypothesis. Lost. But searching.

For now, he will sit inside the WV, his established signal for them to simply please leave him alone. For the hundredth time he wrote definitions college freshman in science should study. He started with theory, then followed with definition of hypothesis, then composed roles that variables play.

Define the Variables

Borrowed from my syllabus notes, revised from graded papers, referenced.

*There should be three categories of **variables** in every experiment: dependent, independent, and controlled.*

***Dependent** -- is what will be measured; what might be affected during the experiment.*

For example, the investigator may want to study plant growth. Possible dependent variables include number of plants, weight of the plant, leaf surface area, time to maturation, height of stem.

***Independent** -- is what is varied during the experiment; what might or will affect dependent variable.*

As amount of fertilizer, type of fertilizer, temperature, amount of H_2O, day length, all of these may affect the number of beans, weight of the plant, leaf area, etc.

Controlled -- the variables that are held constant. See the effect of one independent variable.

Mike hands the paper over to Mary to scrutinize, then asks if she'd agree to present it to Janna and Jude. They will discuss definitions of each word and how it might fit into a study project. He'll build more for them based on how they learn the concepts.

Boy, oh boy. How he missed the classroom.

LUMINSTRATUM

Blue Clear Skies behind David Anthony and My Lady.

David Anthony: *Will I become matter again, ever? I am zeroing in on that, seems every day now! I recognize more aspects about all personalities. Have you heard meaning of the word 'morontial' career?' It's philosophy.*

My Lady: *Yes, I am semi-aware of that group's philosophy. Morontial careers involve spiritual and intellectual development beyond physical existence. Mentorships sometimes. Encompasses connection and eternal improvement. I note how often lately Mary quietly thinks about Dave. How time and space affect love.*

David Anthony: *That, my lady, is truth, yes, for me. The Truth is what people in all places have sought, though each use different rituals. Across all time. Read the texts, files, indexes. All search for it.*

Both David Athony and My Lady, at the same time:

"Truth of Everything does not belong to only or any ONE place or its people. In each language, ALL THE TRUTH, though, even though it is felt and recognized, can't be communicated adequately, for every single language out of more than 7,000 languages is enmeshed and inadequately can convey full meaning and intent. None at 100 percent.

David Anthony: We see and feel truth as love, most always. Love is all that is with us, difficulty is being in the flesh.

Strange Dreams at the WVC

Jude and Janna both dreamt oddly last night.

In Jude's he builds a long, high wall with recycled material sent from scrap yards and junk heaps. He explains to passersby they are houses needing a border — oh, yes, the feds were involved. People laughed, accusatorily, called Jude a divisional racist. Jude just keeps forming, ignoring, biting his tongue.

But upon awakening, Jude makes sure his squibbing captures all he has dreamt.

Yellow Pad Found December 21, 2020.
Professor Merrick. p/45 of 52 (9/20)

Linguistics and culture --- were only some of my electives. One class during those years – maybe it was cultural integration theory -- taught us that souls are to relate to one another. That was not what my dad was paying tuition for and decided to enroll me into a very conservative curriculum

151

at a private school. I was there for a year. I am here, now, as a foreign existence, without a course outline, no curriculum. As usual, the energy moves oddly and faster, the lights are wildly dancing. My instinct: energies are showing something, as though having their own special current purpose.

Janna dreamt a celestial voice whispered in Spanish saying money won't decide a soul's happiness. Their kingdom isn't their house. It's their deeds generated by way of the love they offer. Their kingdom is respected by continual learning. Hone love, the house isn't eternal. Examples are everywhere.

She awoke, sweating, then wrote Squib Book entries quickly. That voice was exactly her mom's who'd passed on, however, in-the-dream her mother's voice spoke in Spanish, a language her mom did not speak, ever know. In the dream Janna perfectly understood meaning, but like her mother, never understood Spanish.

Connected in the dream, she felt her children. All were under this sky, together, holding her newborn babies again. Then her dream shifted. She was driving, screaming, and her kids looked frightened, still in diapers. She yelled out about needing a fair god.

Yellow Pad Found Dec 21,2020.

Professor Merrick. p/ 47 of 52 (9/20)

Entities are preparing something. This is my sense – without support. I remember at WVC, we spoke of Earth souls, interplanetary souls, and Angelic souls. There's belief one's soul

152

immediately leaves the body after the body dies, and if an earthly 'meant to be here' soul flees its encasement, it reincarnates many times. Again, of course, I have no proof. It's highly anti-logic and noncontemporary. The Angelic souls always strive to be helpful. What a vast variety! Different people choose faith and belief in what they decide to carry with them during their life. Again, I don't want to sound like a religious spiritual psychologist goofball, I know. I lately don't recognize myself.

Mary dreamt of the assignment for Meghan and Gracie who'd both giggled while vowing to not forget. 'Beliefs.' Gracie talked about a creator. Meghan smiled, showing two missing teeth. Her dimples were deeper than before, and her eyes twinkled more brightly. "I believe I will see you again, Mama!" she was saying, "My Dad's name is Dave. I know now."

Then the voice of Meghan's dad [a voice now David Anthony's] whispers, "Meghan is being watched over, and will be fine, Mary. She found the recorder of our tapes and knows what she needs to about us." It is his voice, unmistakably deep, kind, with his unique energy she hadn't felt for going on nine years. "She'll grow into a loving and enlightened human being."

The last time she saw her fiancé was when he was opening his questionable business a year after being denied tenure and let go. But about Meghan, in her dream, she felt him the same way she had when they'd fallen in love. She knew now she would not worry any more about Meghan.

Mike dreamt of baseball again. Mickey, Willie, Babe and even Lou were assuring him the cave would be furnished.

Groups of tourists were to visit, they also predicted. Mickey handed him a bat. The dream segued into Mike's attempts to convince the school's administration (which amounted to nine robe-cloaked individuals). They laughed when Mike couldn't form a or accept not having a hypothesis, "You've been opening missing links, huge ones and lots of worm filled cans!"

He calls on his baseball heroes to help persuade and argue with the administration. But their response was, "Welcome to life, we all get handed a tasteless stinky sandwich! Everyone gets skunked. So, what is it that makes you so special? Just Eat It!"

Yellow Pad Found December 21, 2020.
Professor Merrick. p/50 of 52 (9/?/20)

Each time I listen it always becomes a stronger message. The inspiration, the tone, the delivery. I take practically everything that's happened as a spiritual lesson, yes. It is, they are, everything is a lesson. Why do I say this now? I've always known.

Mike's head spun during his next day's trek back to the Detourist cave, now its perfect name. The sun dipped into a variety of silverish orange hues, allowing total darkness. He tried directing his voice toward illuminated areas.

They call but silently. It is to him. They know his soul. He knows he is not insane, unless natural physical pain makes one insane. Still 'they' are unlabeled. Any 'feeling' or 'belief' without evidence is lame, his backbone and gut concur. But he feels them, knows they know him.

What is 'past', still is all 'here and now' - the span of soul existence. Ask moss, for instance, ask mold, ask a caterpillar or a fly. Ask yourself who you were eons ago. It was you. It is you. He scrawls in his notes and has dated and signed, then photographed each yellow page.

154

Exactly what had this experience brought him? He always was being paid. Hardly any curriculum he taught or researched opened this question to him.

Full of awe, love, curiosity, fear, he loathes the thought of being misunderstood. He understood that, just as seas separate continents, people have long been divided by differences like ability and intelligence. But they all question, seek light and truth, then receive the same answers. In different languages.

But humans stayed the same in the biggest way, everywhere! What stays inside, drives them. And they still do:

The search for truth.

He already knew that truth could not belong to only one place, region, continent that was divided by water and belong to only one people, and being misunderstood was like being in hell for him – if there was a hell. He didn't want hell. And he was glad to be a scientist who anticipated the likelihood of flaws yet always planned and had faith and hoped for betterment.

Yellow Pad Found December 21, 2020.
Professor Merrick. p/52 of 52 (9/9/20)

The moon started waning a few days ago. Its light met the cave's wall crevasses. With all the love and hope now inside my heart it was strikingly beautiful, but beautiful for a reason. Two words from two entities rang when approaching. 'Learn More and Be Love' like some rekindled magical belief. Then again, in two other languages, the same result. Then more after that while the music rang with that undeniably same meaning.

But it was so short lived. The beauty in what I saw and heard faded.

Suddenly I saw shapes billowing, like smoke. Nothing was soothing. They weren't peaceful or happy. Decipherability was lost. It stirred me to act promptly - for some reason.

The tiny orbs billowed while turning orange and yellow, then brown. Movement reminded me how fires seem to dance around!

Mike is dizzy, he is hungry. The others were eating crackers, topped with sunflower seeds. Little is left. By avoiding large or second helpings, more rib bones are visible, they're all leaner. Even though they fish, their supply needs to be stretched. There is no clearly expressed fear of dying.

Mike checks their faces, and nobody is gleeful. In the last week he heard remarks from sincere transparency to sarcasm:

"All learned depth we were unaware of before?"

"We are eating less. Doesn't seem like success."

"We've all had to look at our 'authentic self.'"

"Learned we had it good two months ago – and at that time we were thinking we lacked!"

Mike's fingers shake; he has lost his calm.

"Everyone's energy had added to the group's total cohesive awareness. Must be –" Agitated, now and stone-faced, Mike's elbow bangs the table, it nudges his plate. One bean rolls off his plate, followed by several to land on his shoes, then most join the dirt. His cup tips, spilling on his tea on his pants.

Pushing his torso back with one fist, he points with his other to the sky behind their heads. They turn, look.

"That orange skyline above the peaks this morning. Look! Five times bigger now, more orange! See smoke there!"

The others estimate distance, quickly. Mary said two miles, and others said five miles away. Mike wavers.

"This is a major September fire around here."

Quickly he surveys items everywhere in the camp. Within thirty minutes he emptied and moved items into two plastic storage tubs. He strengthens the tugging ropes. "Two people can easily drag," is all he mumbles quickly.

He fills tubs with unperishable food and blankets. Mary watches. She is startled. What were his thoughts? Nobody here could walk a football field's length without pain. Was he going to leave them? Were each of them helpless to figure out what to do?

Purposely silent, he's anxious. He grabs his yellow, blue-lined tablets and slides the lantern to his placemat, claiming his dinner spot. He will be there past dark, he informs. From the trash, he digs out three tin cans, then gathers rolls of foil wrap. From the WV's toolbox, he finds wire, a hammer, a screwdriver, bolts and nails, and then picks out a rock.

He can't talk. All he can think about is that Babe Ruth hit three home runs in Pittsburgh. The final of his 714 career home runs at Forbes field in 1935. He can't pinpoint how or why he thinks of that at all. The others are standing, now, waiting to hear what he tells them to do. They are frightened. Ready.

DECEMBER 23, 2020

Last night as the lodge's fire burned all but two logs, the couple completed reading the entire 52 pages. Each went through the bundle twice. That Michael Merrick had indescribable weeks!

Contacting authorities had been best, and dispatching information on Merrick amassed organizers. All logistics for this sunny day were in place, by seven a.m. Officials, way before midnight had contacted Merrick's closest colleagues – Mary's also, but her missing status had already prompted a need for more interrogation by local officials.

"I am in total amazement how visiting the development turned out so incredibly awe inspiring. The WVC is right next door!" the woman said.

So, a week ago, this trip of the couple's was intended only to check out the status of the developing 3,400 purchased acres and to brief their associates -- located only a mile from the WVC. Now, today, a few more interested investors, consultants and legal officials committed to join. All were short noticed invited to meet at the recently finished commuter airport just one hop and a skip from both the developing property and the WVC area.

Had it been golden luck they'd stepped upon a tin bundle at the WVC? Or not? It was the synchronous call to alert the owner of some unused blocked-off.

A biker, weeks ago, had reported a stranded wrecked van in the middle of it. That is how Rudy Marcher and Dena decided to stop and look at the wreck. Yes, both Rudy and Dena. They were the right couple to find that tin bundle at the right time. Today, from their new commuter airport, all would first caravan to the WVC. After that, some would go on to the development where business affiliates were to be.

Seventeen people. Two county officers, Liam, Ned, and Annella, three sister school foundation professors, two architects, three consultants, two investigators, and Rhetta, Shawna, and....

Drum roll.

"Well, Fawns, good you're all here."

The gathering, upon direction, chose which rental van they wanted to sit in on the trip to the WVC. In one van, the Marchers explained, pointing near the spot where Rudy had, days ago, found the tin wrapped in yellow lined paper. All were informed they'd walked the yards together toward the WVC.

"So, *you* are Merrick's three sister foundation scholars. Glad you can make it with such a short notice!" Dena smiled. The scholars lived an hour's drive from the WVC and found time during the holiday break to join in.

Marcher explained to some of the van load that Merrick's second cousin, Lucille, the young blond lady whose photo Merrick had slid inside the pads, when contacted about Merrick had become ecstatic. She'd eventually fly in, saying she was tending to his pets, and how badly they were missing him.

Weeks before, Shawna with Rhetta together eagerly met when the Marchers positioned them with Gina. Titles and responsibilities were assigned but were still in negotiation. Rhetta's detailed research report had paralleled aspects of the Marcher's. Dena had already assumed the wise Rhetta suspected some minor spying but believed it wouldn't affect future trust.

The gifted jeep had shaken Rhetta up weeks ago, but she'd persisted that morning with Rudy, all through breakfast and lunch, flagging points in her research, sometimes pushing data in at face after seeing his memorably odd driveway performance.

While eating together, an hour later, his eyes were fixated on hers, as though trying to read her mind, and then they became glued to hers, for ten minutes. He listened for hours, turned and read pages.

It was great compiled research. He'd at once, while at the restaurant table, dialed up Dena who then was in the recreation room at the nursing home. She'd then decided to ditch the social resident chit-chat hour to quickly summon Shawna's abilities to cyber-meet hookup help.

"Seems spot on!" aligned with the Marcher philosophies and concerns. Seeds are similar! This will be concrete!"

All were energized. What would this day show them?

Rudy helped Dena out of the van, set her carefully in her wheelchair amidst warming sighs. He wrapped two woolly scarves around her neck, placed her sunglasses on her ears securely, and then clipped its chain to her collar. Dena smiled, then joked a whisper, "My Star Power needs to have someone fetch my pills and some water!"

Then she kindly motioned Shawna for help.

Many hours for sunlight were needed. Better hurry.

Rhetta wore her happiest face, still not knowing a thing about who Merrick was, she'd been briefed about a bundle found and a van wreck beside a camp that had a college professor, a librarian, and two others. She was to be there simply to lead the development party to explain property plans and areas.

"I was planning to visit you at Gardenia later on in November, Dena, but so ran out of time! Glad we had the cyber meet ups... Did I tell you I sold the jeep? Needing now to know exactly why you gifted it - oddest of all! The gesture motivated me like a shovel. I dove quickly into analyzing!"

160

"Rhetta," Dena let go of her hands. "We've lots of work to do together!"

"I sent to your office a copy of the jeep's check. It shows I donated that money to help the community center" It was toward the same causes Dena had been noted to support. Looking forward to working with you and Rudy! So very much!"

"I hear it had 43 miles on it!" Rudy smiled. Accountability was king with the Marchers.

Shawna handed Dena the pills and the water, patted her back, then shot Liam a warming glance.

Immediately smitten with Shawna, Liam knew. His first glimpse of her six weeks before at the Gardenia Senior Home while she cared for his mother woke something up in him. He'd asked her to a yacht party, she declined, but he'd kept trying to speak to her.

At one yacht party he watched his sister, Annella, glue her eyes to a long-term care intern named Rory. He'd applied for a job within the development. Once Rory saw the Illumed senior home blueprints, he explained himself imaginatively during a Marcher trademarked casual dinner interview.

Dena affirmed with Rudy that their kids would soon be highly aware of what assets they no longer would have. They'd need to be trained if they wanted to be part of this project. Trained inclusiveness, not nepotism. There were no guarantees for their future there. Build on what they have left.

A new phase would start next week, digging multi-storied deep basements, and then, like a puzzle, fit other components. Many opportunities would unfold. Dena's and Rudy's philanthropic dreams would manifest, foster more growth, center on cultural needs – all would be self-sustaining.

SURVEYING THE WVC

Enriched emerald-green trees with December's snow undressing it by melting in clumps, like a white sun-lit mink dance. The September fire had closed in from the opposite direction. It had burned right up to the Marcher's property.

Dena sensed the fire must have been stopped by some bossy spirit, a secret for itself. It knew -- to *just stop it already*!

If anyone heard her thoughts, she'd be labeled loony, she knew. All her bones felt the mild wakening chill of a spirit. Closing nearer, and parking, many pairs of feet began to crunch upon rocks and snow. Their chatter, like cloudy frosted speech balloons, quieted in a domino chain the very second each person saw to feel the wrecked van.

A mystical, sacred, sad tone of abandonment joined their mood. Those who knew Merrick realized the pearly white was a short-lived prize Mike designed for his sabbatical van.

Inside a toppled wreck,a metallic musky scent filled Rudy's nostrils. Late autumn rain had caused mildew. There weren't crumbs or wrappers or empty jars. Nothing in its cupboards except spider webs, dead bugs, and a few sandwich bags full of coffee grounds or fish bones. If bedding or clothing at one point existed, all was gone. Inside the fridge a puddle of murky water showed ice had formed and thawed several times over.

Rudy remembered to check for the extra cell phone inside the glove compartment, following what Merrick had noted to the finder to do. An empty juice bottle rested on a dried blooded passenger seat, giving proof a life once smelled the same 'new car smell' that was still there, in the present. Outside, Dena, undiscouraged though shivering, peered through sharded

162

windshield and felt the same horror Merrick and Hawkings had shared last August.

No cell phone was where it should have been. Rudy unfolded a damp note with smeared ink which read *'if looking for a phone, likely it's with me at the other place'* in a hurried scrawl.

This could be good.

Perhaps one attempted hundreds of times to connect – then voila, had succeeded? Two new cell towers were stationed near the commuter airport – both could send a radius of 61 miles. An operating phone would succeed by the first of December. No call was tried, though, the records showed.

The solar panel generator showed no damage. Probably, though, it hadn't been used in months. A damaged cell phone cord was beside it. Marcher recalled reading the 52 pages Merrick thrice said he was solar power recharging cells.

Enough time to check the copter? Not today.

More importantly, they needed to first find that hill cave. Tower trucks, it was suggested, should be scheduled to visit. Maybe load the copter, later the van, but special officials first needed to deeply investigate details inside each.

They knelt. That summer's grassy knolls now had snow. Dena whispered, "that dear man." Dr. Michael Merrick, in the late summer, had rested his aching head there, had recorded hearing the magic, seeing sights. A rusting fire pit sat near the cave entry, housing two small frying pans and one pot. No visible food particles. Four smooth, low rocks surrounding the pit. All were seeking shelter there likely sat for warmth, cooking and eating, planning and perhaps praying, too.

Alongside the pit a pan sat ready to be scrubbed. The van's stove rack was carried over. Stiff sponges and iced gloves hung off a closed soaked address book which rested on a dry erase board. Crayola markings spelled four names and the days of the week/and times listed: "*Shower/Sponge Bath Schedule*".

Dena didn't miss a thing. A wire basket held pounded down tin cans, hammers, rocks, wire and foil. A metal tray had three blank Squib booklets ready for an author to record their thoughts. Inside, plastic food storage containers held thirty books, full of writing. A separate adjacent container contained a significantly larger quantity.

A yard from the cave's entranceway, a closed suitcase waits, packed with twenty Squib Books, wrapped in foil. They are thicker than the 52-paged one which Marcher had found. "*Janna, Jude,* or *Mike*' are inked upon the front of each one.

Translucent, whitish butterflies flitted about the brush. Five owls of white, brown, black, tawny, and gold each had preselected their own branch to scrutinize the small procession of these newer people.

Their nonstop gaze studied these humans today. All who are clad differently and moved with assured demeanor -- not looking to protect themselves. The last bunch is not so assured.

All the owls understood using their vibrational frequency. A part of the order. Whatever is felt is radiated back. Not understood, though, were entire meanings or intentions. Humans survive in their own way. A grand show to watch daily.

If owls could talk to humans, they would say how could they miss noticing all the masses of tiny moving particles? It's around them constantly traveling over and through, above and behind them. The particles have spirit in them.

164

The owls' eyes follow those bits, night and day. Some humans, though, do notice something passing around and through. They'd whisper to fields of energy. 'Spirit' or 'ghost' are sounds at times uttered.

Marchers asked a few others with them to become quieter to listen to details of nature. Merrick's group likely had witnessed and may have felt. Dena felt the energy of prayers. She began to cry. The owls watched. Three of them closed their gazing eyes.

Falling snow hit the departing vans that would be approaching the development. Liam and Ned follow Shawna and Rhetta like puppies would their mamas. These girls are super smart with a depth neither of the boys had yet experienced.

Brevity became the wide order to family, partners and the Board. Questions by onlookers would eventually be responded to. Also, for the WVC, blanket phrases of 'all statuses were being legally reviewed.' meant skillful skimming of generalities.

Both the WVC and the cave already contributed inspiring depth to the Marcher's new property, a community they'd been designing. These brought intrigue, should likely draw in. Both Marchers became more overawed per second.

But guard strongly what now the development is aimed for - guard info that wasn't yet prepared for public knowledge.

Rudy and Dena stood alone, waving goodbye to the other two of Merrick's colleagues who'd only visited to view the camper and cave area. They'll take the newly paved road, which finished last October, connecting highways, nine miles each way.

"We need to find the cell phones, at least Merrick's."

Who would venture later that day into the cave? Rudy hoped the officials would find life tomorrow or the next day, though it felt unlikely the injured four survived, even with fish they'd froze or animals they might have sling shot and cooked.

Rudolf Marcher calls loudly into the cave. Then again, louder, but he only hears his echo, no response. Dena also tries, thinking a weak vibration might capture living attention. They each venture seven more yards into it and try again.

LUMINSTRATUM

David Anthony: *My Lady, my ladies, all the ladies and gentlemen will hear many soothing ideas, and their purpose is to serve. Serving dear, dear sweetness to these hearts.*

My Lady: *Someone remains special to you. When you query questions, music in spirit. A memory of your heart. At least one of us, David Anthony, is in a morontia existence. I think it is you.*

David Anthony: *Clear of that, yes. A new mission here in Illumined Town. I will be in matter, in flesh somehow for some reason at the Illumined senior Home. I want to please the residents in the Illumined Home. My voice and the maker's words in their ears. I like to say, they are spirit melodies.*

44:0.3 (497.3) The celestial artisans are not created as such; they are a selected and recruited corps of beings composed of certain teacher personalities native to the central universe and their volunteer pupils drawn from the ascending mortals and numerous other celestial groups. ..... Spirit melodies in one religious philosophy aren't material sound waves, but spirit pulsations received by spirits of celestial personalities. It is wholly beyond human comprehension, this spirit's energy.

(Partial citing from The Urantia Book, Paper 44)

166

Chapter SEVEN

SOME YEARS LATER

So. Where did the first visitors come from, and how?

During Phases One and Two, they came from Oregon, Washington, California, Utah, and Idaho, then trickled from Nevada. Word of mouth worked. Relatives and friends took the reviews and made sure they'd visit that *Illumined Town* place!

By Phase Three, the place hummed. National travel blogs touted, *'Stay in the area at least three days!'* and *'check fantasy deer statues on the grounds! Visit the rooftops! Conversations will start! Might enlighten!*

Parts of their vast basements will open to the public! And do make time to visit the Illumined Senior home residents who are simply intriguing.

What do you know or care about Deer Art?

How does your grandmother reallllly think? Go listen to or read her amusing literature at The Illumined Library!

'Illumined Town fawns all over the place. Up to you. Check it!'

Blogs and guidebooks and travel agents glorified. They all direct drivers to look for an offramp 'Very Deer Road' glide left onto 'Very Deer Way' to drive along colorful gardens lined by sculptured deer bushes. Turn north at 'Dearest Deer Circle.' Bronze sculpted luxury gates wrapped in lit orb shapes greet all.

"But wait! All newcomers would park and quickly disembark and be just as curious as the next, more often - due to word-of-mouth-about *that mystery*.

"Ever learn about the stranded campers?"

"I heard rumors: it's a bit of fun nonsense. This town is unlike anything I've ever visited."

"Heard there's a bit of woo woo."

"Well, that brings it more attention. I want to know what they plan to do with the gate code data!"

Few know monthly how much the number of visitors increased, *Apply online for gate codes, it's a rule.'* Discern origins of groups and reasons why they've visited.

'WHAT is the REAL reason they visit.'

"Understand how, why, when and what motivates them!" became a mission of the Board of Directors.

Earlier, during Phase One, all outer structure walls were squeezed out quickly. 3-D printing sand and cement pours - layered and dried in just three or four days! The digital fabrications encased nursing/assisted living quarters, then painted a soft blue, which complemented fountain-sculptures of deer families surrounding a beautiful pond with ferns, lilies and narcissus foliage, ivy and of all things, hemp!

"Why the deer?"

"Thematically, I suppose, maybe because the community carries a philosophy or mode. Deer qualities symbolize perfection, intuition, messenger, grace, divinity, compassion, renewal, spirit growth, and especially, *CYCLES OF LIFE AND DEATH.*"

'The' photo op spot drew wheelchaired patients and family visitors who were convinced to say 'cheese' at that spot. A loving

168

place to be nursed, the Illumined Senior Home! Patient applications piled in from more states, then applicant forms were first screened to meet requirements. One must have been surviving for 11.5 years at a lower middle-class income. A clean background check was essential.

The first quarter filled 257 beds out of the full 430 capacity

"To qualify, one must be for 11.5 years at a lower middle-class income. It is enormous. Huge. A clean background check is also needed."

"Photos from the fountain ops are printed on postcards. There are selfies! Their brand is *P.S. I love you Fawnies*! How cool is that? And the paper they're on is processed on site!"

"Oh! Look! Window boxes of narcissuses! That's a lovely hemp plant bordering them? Can't be hallucinatory!"

"Narcissuses are replaced by pinecone sprouting during colder months, I read that. Masses of hemp and menthol here."

Acres between, another beautiful pour boasted formidable condominiums (with window boxes). Pastel green with teal trimmed beauty on seven levels! (Five above ground, two below).

Each of the 230 condo home units were built providing each owner(s) a view of a sculpted vegetation pond site with statuettes of fawns, owls, squirrels, and coyotes peek from a bush. These scenic areas surrounded each condo building.

The 'Dearest Fallow Store' is huge. It is to sell naturally grown food, 70% grown on the Marcher's land, and its 'Dearly Deer Inns' were to be accommodative. Two cafes on the top floor: Doe Mojo, and Buck Brew, were doing great.

"Let's caffeinate! I had too much county wine last night!"

All rooftops had greenhouses and solar panels. Here, visitors sat by the chimneyed fire pits to view various angles of the beautiful country below. They'd photograph mountains and forests in every season. Serendipitous conversations reliably titillated 100% provocative. Be quiet and just peer through one of four donations - mounted telescopes with names of learning institutions engraved on them. Spot the constellations!

Visitors sought visitors. Where to be after dinner? On the rooftops! Inside and outside dining areas and all the menu and management were provided by Captain Halbert. He was the boss! And he *loved* listening to people share more whopping tales, working on his third book, all about the whopping tales! Another reason to return to Illumined Town: Hear and be heard, share to be shared. Talk about what you want to talk about.

"A travel blog said two campers from that 2020 campsite wreck once rented a hotel room. A Janna and a Jude?"

"I just heard someone worked caricatures while his wife walked around with a poetry book she'd written -- about love and beauty and souls inside their body houses. The guy illustrated it."

"I heard the story of them being here was a fake."

"Well, I am trying to find out if their book exists."

Inside the condominiums and the Inn, exclusive elevators were built - apart from elevators transporting to quarters' floors. The delegated main one connected only to rooftop floors and basement floors, skipping residential quarter areas. All basements had doors to underground tunnels.

"Tunnels are decorated with printed framed copies of Jude Art, and photos of WVC artifacts. Lots of references regarding Squib Books, whatever those are."

Solar paneling was on every rooftop along with

greenhouses and a few other innovative structures. Basements had small theaters, a library housed cyber copies of ALL Squib books, many written by nursing home patients.

What needed boasting, though, was a stand-alone seven-storied thermal greenhouse! (two stories underground). Bunches of narcissus. Greens, tomatoes, citrus and much else grew.

"Did you hear what took the trees down at that WVC? I heard it was a meteorite responsible for the wreck."

"Nobody knows … or very few do. Well, I don't know."

"That Jude guy's rhinestone copter blade patio dangler piece – is not for sale, it's encased. See corridor basements."

"There's a lot in the hemp corridors now!"

"Yes. Given its very own set-apart acre of storied greenhouses, hemp is the word there, big time. Greenhouses there display celestial beauty art in its narrow corridors. Many pieces of refurbished recycled artwork dangle while catching all light. Atop were solar panels and a telescope, too!"

"Some bear Jude Juniper's signature. Great cool name!"

Not only did hemp produce more oxygen than forests, but more cellulose, biofuel, and textiles – all critical to a mission of Illumined Town. Here, mainly, it's processed into paper!

"Was it hemp paper pushing the Illumined Library to add rooms? Did hemp factor into paying for dorm housing -- for college students who were helping the elderly? Explain!"

"It's due to the elderly heart, and the listener's heart Board's directive they get heard, written, read."

This is the main tale. Its reality began during the first weeks of move-ins. Assisted living and nursing home custodial patients had been expressing deep, saddening lonesomeness.

Somebody, anyone? Sit beside me for a while? Their eyes and faces plead, please listen to my truth!' Soon gravitation toward them occurred. Truly all were oddly interesting!

Filled with love and sorrow fostered for a lifetime, heaviness of memory's energy sought a landing place.

Illumined Town's hemp paper debuted and too soon growing clutches of regular eager listeners began to hear and write, and repeatedly visit the patients. Outpourings of true stories were reported as being cathartic.

"You'll hardly believe what these grandmothers, in most cases, held in their minds!"

Minds stacked with innuendo, crime and love, adventure and mystery. Listeners took notes! And more notes, composed, edited then collaborated. They published. On that hemp paper!

Fast forward, the numbers of visitors, volunteers and students grew. Illumined Town's Board of Directors arranged bartering contracts to foster this growing need. Hemp paper.

College chancellors voted 'yes.' The nursing students could be credited for overarching electives! English and Journalism students got wind of that elective, too!

Then Psychology and Sociology.

'Interviewing the Elders' began. Student writers and readers and assemblers of Elderly Personalized Squib Books installed themselves, then a newspaper and a public service television documentary picked up on this 'mission to listen.'

"Hey, I hear there is a Dr. Mike who comes around at night and sets something on bedstand tables. You hear that?"

"Yes, a hemp greeting card with his signature and his lady friend Mary's signature."

"But I heard neither have been seen entering or leaving."

"That's similar to the story people claim to have spotted the Juniper lady fixing patient hair and make-up, shaving some."

"The card messages are directly to each patient, such as 'Mrs. Smith, a part of you will always live on in others' and 'people here love you, Jack, and want to hear about your life.'"

"The treat to ALL men and women custodial patients was a very sweet and caring telephone love call from David Anthony and My Lady. One of them would call, spend fifteen minutes every three days, and speak to each woman and man. They knew them, somehow, as if the person's maker would, as angels."

"That's so silly."

"No, all of them testify that they get a phone call that soothes them with lullabies, sometimes seductively, I hear, but nobody is truly complaining. They all stay happy."

Bedtime was a lot of the time. Anytime, it was always at bedtime. Many of them requested to have their tv's turned off for fifteen minutes. They wanted to hear Anthony's voice sooth them, or My Lady's voice encourage them.

Story coordinators neared brinks of notoriety. Public service angles amplified. The 'poor unqualified for state aid' were now adequately served, and the home and hemp paper became another philanthropic tool and media spotlight.

"So, now a trendy internship for students nationwide?"

173

"Apparently! Students can dorm for a quarter or semester."

Many courses within community college curriculum were rearranged to meet the required attributes of how course-outlined lessons were to be taught by cyber, or face to face.

"Wow, watch that classic online class recording regarding the psychology of the elderly by social psych Dr. Merrick. He taught a decade ago. He's the prof whose van got hit by a tree."

Overarching and new catch all's articulated electives, malleably fitting within majors and disciplines: Geriatrics, Multiculturism, Botany, Critical Thinking, Reading, Writing, Selective Attention, Logic, Interviewing, English, Nursing, Psychology, Sociology.

The tales of the forgotten and the economically challenged fueled a richness during medicine and juice times. Newest topics ranged: 'wanting to be famous' '16 kids' 'advice to the young' 'wanting to make love to someone,' 'affairs,' 'saving someone's life' 'babies given up' 'school at 55' 'divorcing' 'poems' 'who I really loved' 'learned too late' 'narcissists like me are ok.'

Name it, they said it, 'who I didn't know well until they died.' 'others who never realized I didn't like one thing about them.'

At first their bold, unembellished expressions caused discomfort among staff and visitors. The patients were growing fearless. Nobody could scare them much anymore.

Within a hop-an-a-skip and an-a-jump from the beds, worked a Board of Directors who cared deeply about them.

The Illumined Library's Elderly Squib Books had national circulation code headers for the Senior Citizen: shopping, praying, doubting, family, friends, nursing homes, David Anthony, My Lady, assisted living, libido, believing, memory, funerals, maladies, angels, best jobs and worst, children who decades later looked them up.

'Three illuminators for every darkness are truth, nature, knowledge.' was embossed on each first page of blank hemp Squib booklets.

"They sell blank Squib Books at the gift post card place. Their brand name is: *'Blankety Blank Fawning Hemp Books.'*"

"Those four campers wrote a LOT while inside that cave. Proof of that is in the Illumined Library. Cyber copies only. "

"You look through some thickened glass in the main building to see some original WVC Squib Books."

"I want to see Dr. Merrick's 52 lined, yellow page one."

"They won't be loaned out. One stays there to read even a copy on their private website. While being checked. A lot is on their private cyber line."

Retirees, artists and writers would picnic, sit and write; the others drew or painted. People learned Deer Symbology. All enterers were handed a constantly updated map. All smiled. Nobody remained lost. People walked up to strangers, received the latest scoops. People sure were creative with their tales.

Every few weeks brought more new questions regarding the WVC fate, which answers given only morphed rumors to be spread. The creativity of tales increased.

Mystery shrouded WVC's reality and campers' futures.

"Not all towed away, sites were being restored after investigations were finished."

"The wrecked van was plexi-glassed. The cave was not available for the public until a later phase but photos inside of how it was found were hung in the foyer of the BOD."

"That's advised by scholars and lawyers to not allow people to open anything in the foyer. Safety and theft reasoning given."

"When nothing's verified, nothing offers clarity."

"Lured in," the skeptics opined, "Oh, my, the mystique, silly me. If we know more, and I mean 'more factoids' - before we leave town -- it's lunch on me at Lumi Café."

"Next time we come. If we come."

"Let's go watch them make hemp paper over wine!"

"I hear people can enroll into classes next spring on hemp shoe design, construction - and purses and textile!"

Illumined Town became a blueprint for developers. Authors, librarians, artists, and scholars visited. Support flowed in: Donations, opinion, advice, barter, and unprecedented amounts of interest in volunteering.

Newest opinions of engineers, and liberal industrialists planned to donate time to create 'chunnel's' for chickens (screened tunnels to prohibit predators). "They strut and naturally fertilize rectangular patches of vegetable gardens. Then they lay eggs inside an adjoining solar warmed hutch."

Another idea was to steer streams from the nearby mountains' melting snow, create canals with solar panels. This would save on water and generate gigawatts of clean energy.

Specialists and textile cultivators began to plan small field trips to see instructional sessions – while sipping county wine and listening to live music - on how to treat and process the fiber, this deeply odd plant. Visitors watched hemp fibers go into the blender, layered to dry in trays. Wine bottles were labeled with hemp paper, decorated by volunteer local artists.

176

Everyone, all day, walked in seemingly magic spells, and the shyest would suddenly want to meet and strike conversations with new acquaintances. Many felt warmth, a celestial feeling, a spirit of love.

Hundreds of acres nearby were ready for more.

Three foundations were headed by Officer Rhetta Marcher, yes, that's correct, Mr. Ned Marcher and Mrs. Rhetta Marcher. They'd married after six months of dating. Dena 88% accepted them. Ned received no salary until the board approved whether the weight of his stated commitments met his actual contribution.

Besides that, they were expecting twins.

The Marcher Family Trust had been altered. Initially, he'd been okay with it (on the condition that Rhetta would marry him). So far, his effort was remarkable, a magnificent change flowed through him, people felt it.

Both he and his siblings continued monitoring the corporate and government grants which helped fund 1. Fifty-five years and up ages would be receiving housing and long-term care, and 2. education, production and training for recycled products, and 3. the knowledge-bank storing meta data – all to gain exponential growth every month.

Shawna and Liam were dating. Together they remained responsible for the nursing home and its medical assistant education center. Their small staff helped coordinate education centers. All existing acreage on the north side was aimed toward onsite housing, training, and employing of the lower income.

Migrant education and training along with assisting families in surrounding areas provided affordable childcare. Always, they worked to negotiate with foundations and billionaires who weren't always on the same page. (Fast forwarding: hope was cut for future recipient federal funding by Phase Seven.)

Annella and her fiancée had, for the first year, worked in their sole building on the south side. Their daunting task was to decipher and repair many 'after-the-discovery' Squib Booklets of Mike's, Mary's, Jude's and Janna's. All 142 originals were encased on the top floor of the BOD administration offices of Illumined Town, with many photographs and biographies.

Mike's cousin, Lucille Michaels, (née Merrick), had moved from Southern California, a short mile from where Merrick had lived, bringing the adopted Merrick's pets. She'd become immediately emotional in 2021 when told all what Mike and his other campers had endured.

And she'd became smitten with the idyllic Illumined Town.

She bought a flat on each floor of both condominiums by the end of Phase Seven. None seemed to dare ask this private woman, why she had done this, nor knew the area of her profession. Able to afford 14 homes was over-the-top unusual. But people watched her, followed her, and all reported nobody ever saw items or furniture she owned inside.

Mary Hawking's daughter, Meghan and the Land family began visiting Lucille at the Illumed Inn Hotel. Once Meghan began loving to visit there, Lucille offered the Land family access to one of her seven homes. They brought sweet Meghan.

Lucille was ultra guarded; it was widely a supposition that she supported Mary's daughter, Meghan, and was attending to details of guardianship, alongside Gracie's mom, Mrs. Land. Also, it was believed she had paid for Meghan's higher education. Apparently, someone from the college where Merrick and Mary worked revealed this after vacationing Illumined Town. Someone spread information that the visiting colleague had lengthy discussions about Mike and Mary with the BOD. This reportedly brought possibility of credulity.

But of course, it was another loose flying possibility, nobody verified it.

Lucille was often noted to walk a short distance inside a connecting tunnel between the condo's basements, landing into the community room gymnasium where at times she was seen swimming, wearing a full-bodied black swimsuit, and bringing her magazines. Merrick's dog would be with her, everywhere. A few visitors and other condo owners successfully peeked when she'd bend over, dialing the cell number of that Mike Merrick's, *that missing social psychologist professor.'*

She would hold his cell to the dog's ear to hear Merrick's recorded outgoing message. People reported hearing, "Hi, it's Mike Merrick. I'm away right this minute, but…."

Rumors swirled about lady Lucille. Was she *really* related to a WVC person? Speculation created probing. People thought she knew *all* the answers. Was that why she seemed standoffish? Quietly, she held on to more questions than they did.

She grew gleeful when watching his dog's tail wag at the sound of Mike's voice. It was what she needed, daily.

Two huge fireplaces lined the inside pool walls. People spotted her on the condominium rooftops, peering through telescopes, studying luminous moon phases. If approached for friendly conversation, she would tap upon the telescope, "this telescope was donated by the university's astronomy department," and communicate with stern facial expressions she'd not join chit chat nosiness.

The scent of decorative menthol and production hemp wafted every night, creating a haven for star watchers. Paper demand exponentiated.

Published copies of Senior Squib Books branched into the county at large. Any profit was reinvested in the Illumined Town or voted for specificity - to help wider communities around.

So, it is now asked, and often, by almost too many:

"What did two Marchers find from that cave visit in December 2020?" and "Were owls and butterflies really surrounding the recovery crews?"

What was the full and complete truth? What happened and when to the WVC four? BOD lips were sealed.

Enough people knew that on December 23, 2020, the cave was stamped as a landmark, just as the WVC had been. Without full disclosure, people jabbered and zeroed in on newest tales.

"Had the cell phone of Merrick been recovered? Were the four ever spotted around Illumined Town?"

"Were any of them found?"

And this: "What were the campers doing with some of those feathers inside of the cave?" Those questions arose the moment people learned of Jude's artwork. On his bark cutting, he'd used many of those feathers. His artwork was displayed next to the larger, intricately patterned wings, all prominently encased in the administration's office foyer

The foyer had a cubed perimeter of offices with wooden doors. The name plaques of Merrick, Hawkings and each of the Junipers were permanently attached to the locked doors. And it was unknown when anyone would have permission to see their insides. "What was inside? Why were the doors always locked?"

"Why is this all so secret?"

"Did you know they tried to quelch that rumor how

someone saw that Mike Merrick talking to the patients, and how that Mary was seen walking around the care home, leaving custodial patients greeting cards? The rumor couldn't be stopped because cards kept on being found on their bed tables!"

"Surveillance didn't record either Mike or Mary on tape, however, videotape records exist with patients smiling and glowing while reading newest bed table laid cards."

Very few, less than five people, knew answers to many questions. Others could be answered by lawyers and scholars who continually found reasons to quelch, always providing nebulous answers. Strongly, they kept their lips tight. A classic

On any curious or sleepless night.

No matter who asked, all received the same filtered P.R. explanation: "Yes, the four remain under case study. And no, a full disclosure is unavailable; still, too much is unknown.

Responses were simply, "We don't know either." And, or "What we know is what *only we know.*" "IYKYK" "Not wise to join the Delulu club. Gotta leave now!"

"Don't the missing people receive a fair deal legally, to be investigated thoroughly for public knowledge?"

All the Four's Squib Books continued to be deciphered by scholars who held part time residence on the acreage in exchange for their services. And they were also provided with Illumed Town home grown groceries and hemp paper for life.

"But why do people keep saying that Janna and Jude own a beauty shop in the basement of the senior nursing quarters?"

"If they're all dead, and if all this is rumored nonsense, at least some closure could be provided for the public! Like, how long did each survive, or wait around, or …?"

The only public information (thought as fact) was this: "A huge bundle of beautiful feathers had been located inside the cave. That is evidence of the campers' connection to the feathers. Nobody knew how to answer those questions, like, "what living vertebrae at one time had worn those wings?"

Eventually visitors could be told the number of books written by the WVC people. Most of the books' contents continually were examined. Each camper, as it now was known, while at WVC followed by three months in the cave, had recorded thoughts, their own truths. Their journeys, their letters and essays, their plans, their desires, their questions, their grace, and their expressed anger.

All were well recorded.

Cave art, by Jude. He carved using knives, colored with blood and pastels. There were traces of food, mostly fishbones.

And most interesting of all, it was public that one very precious page of Merrick's written paper had become available for reading. It was loose from the 52-page bundle. But written for whom? It became framed and encased beside the feathers.

Volunteers and paid staff performed at optimal efficacy. Because of this, Illumined Town community became viewed by other national areas as prototypic, reaping feedback responses regarding its self-sustenance having a culture geared toward the betterment of social concord, common good, education, self-nurturing, efficacy. With cleanest energy, care and commitment!

Clear communication was to be frequent, spelled with an 'F', and many of the Board Members murmured how goals were to keep the **Fawning Frequency** alive.

Rate at which a vibration occurs which constitutes a wave, either in a material (as in sound waves), or in an electromagnetic field (as in radio waves and light), usually measured per second.

Isn't *that* just fawning fantastic?

Yes, frequency. The Board Members used a room in their area, only for themselves, to meditate in. Each could enjoy a window seat designed by Rhetta - a replica of the window seat she'd used while in New York where she'd studied research for the Marchers to propel the plan of Illumined Town.

The Board voted to name the room, *My Lady and Anthony* Each window seat had a phone installed, just for them to talk to either Anthony or to My Lady. All the board members' faces kept the broadest smiles known of in the area.

Presumption in the community was to conduct oneself with 'the' attitude of meliorism (practice perceiving the present moment to be perfect) and not to assign blame.

Find your gratitude.

How could complete gratefulness occur when explanations would rarely be valid. Nor would arrive after a group of visitors spent an afternoon session in either the Illumined Town Nursing Home, the Hotel, the Dining Roof, or the library, when being very touched, they'd still claim conclusiveness. Unchecked, mostly.

"Hey, but! So, apparently there's truth in their writings and their experiences and the public can digest that fact and weigh it. But, the truth, please!"

"When it happens, we will get word. I think they are alive – at least the social psychologist still is, right? Or not? Maybe, he's hiding from the current government who despises professors! – ha. My joke for the day. The librarian lady is hiding, too!"

"Who would in their right mind accept that each

183

from the WVC had 'emerged from the cocoon, then floated from their own house?'"

"Did they persist within themselves, intact, whether as a spirit or soul or some other unknown energy? Do I sound like a meta groupie?"

"Well, that's a beginning, not an ending. I think all of this is fabrication, amazing. Some candied crap."

"Oh, but those tragic crashes, the struggles, the truths are written! Vanished, surreal!

Most of the readers and speculators figured when Merrick first saw the fire to December 23rd, perhaps that span was enough to survive if enough food. No trace of bodies, yes, but perhaps they made it to safety after healing - having eaten enough to stay alive. And find a remote place to heal? Completely heal? Surely it could be a sweet story's new beginning.

"Did they lose their memory and therefore their identity? Are they unconscious or have they forgotten who they are, and have no communicative ability? Rehabilitating somewhere? Not a good ending or an adequate start for a new beginning."

"See, just a bunch of malarky."

But the researcher's diamonds were Merrick's two cell phones; they were wrapped in plastic, hiding in pillowcases.

The detached, or loosened, a yellow, blue-lined page with a hanging stapled laid alone. Assumingly, it was from the original bundle of 52 other pages, and found beside the cell phones in plastic, never tin-wrapped, it was alone. The important page.

Merrick, it was agreed, had signed it. (see on page 188-189)

Each cell phone was also wrapped in plastic having blank yellow paper taped with notes written, showing four different sets of handwriting, trying to either sound out or spell foreign words! Some words later translated into English's *'The Way'* and *'The Truth'*. The original finders guessed correctly that cells had photos and voice recordings likely of the cave visits.

"So, if any of the four 'luminary wrecked van campers' are alive, then they are living near this area?"

"Wouldn't that just be the case to give closure to it! And they are living happily ever after! I mean, no death discovered!"

"But there are so many variables to formulate an argument, and the twisty logic doesn't work to solve the problem. Isn't that just the truth of the method? No argument there, right?"

The consensus given out by the county officials said all rumors had been generated by only tidbits of info. An inadequate amount of info was still being qualified and evaluated, needing more reliable evidence. Facts - in publication form, would be/ are signed by the Board of Directors.

Many wisely remained quiet, realizing all shared thoughts not only were disrespectful, but what they thought was unconfirmed, received through unreliable grapevines .... or:

"Ones who talked to me who mentioned [this or that] went to college. They don't share anything out of the ordinary for the purpose of getting attention."

"Oh, ever? Care to form a group, go over it. Will there be a cult, a subcult, a sect?"

Others imagined how the four escaped, got help, and then became healed somehow. Then they'd return.

The Board of Directors asked individuals in the wider communities to stop spreading UNVERIFYABILITY, i.e. "TALES" in this town should DISCONTINUE. Our wonderful community must not frighten. No propelling fear.

"Because no haunted villages can survive."

"Yes, there'd be no mail deliveries or businesses with a sane secure person working - if those tales were true…."

"Semi agreeing. But on the flip side, once determined, the actual number of weirdos who visit is because they love spooky melodramas. Draw, not deter."

Whenever an Illumined employee repeated some form of what they'd heard, they'd eventually face the directors who would then, with sage-like aura, kindly re-set, then guide with pragmaticism to dissuade superstition and propagation.

Scholars and Lawyers and other scientists and hired officials dedicated to truth chose to volunteer the scrutiny effort. Every finding was weighed for validity and ramifications. When a case was found not to be evidence-based, it should not be shared. But putting a lid on it was challenging.

Curiosity continued to attract all kinds of tourists, though.

But the latest of the newest 'theories' was 'perhaps one or two in the WVC group, were hanging around here alive and well, and worked anonymously - probably operating 'in some disguise' and 'too sensitive to let the secret be known!'

Conjectures became a flunked logical problem:

"If not alive, then at least bones would be found!"

"Not necessarily, dummy. What did you miss out of while in school?"

Rumors bolted after visitors got wind of reports, for instance, that inside the seven-floor condominium structure a beautiful chiming bell and beautiful surreal sounding songs were occasionally heard, *"emitting from...where? the ceiling?"*

"Who said that?"

"I don't know, I just heard someone heard."

"Although I am embarrassed to share anything, or entirely believe anyone or anything, EVER again ... let me tell you. Honestly, no kidding, I swear on a Bible from any religion there is. I HEARD BELLS and saw owls and butterflies the other day while inside there."

Belief and trust became more abstract as people grew enthralled, addicted, entertained by complexity. Wanting news. People began questioning anybody's words regarding the WVC survivors. Or non-survivors.

"Since my colleague [he or she] is always reliable and knows a lot, then what she says must be more likely real and true! She says that they're alive."

One interesting partially verified fact: The voices of Anthony (*verified as Dave's*) and My Lady made their way into Lucille's cellphone. But nobody knew about that. And Lucille once mentioned she spoke to a boyfriend two times per day.

"Well, then how did you find out about the voices, then. Did you dream it up? Lucille doesn't speak to anybody."

"No, it's true!"

And so, let it be true. But let it be true and factual. And full of Hope. Be Love. Follow The Way. Select your Faith. Amen

"Don't pray about it. Tell me the damned truth!"

"Just be cool with it. Go have some wine on the roof"

The Loose Paper of Merrick, Found In Cave

A loosened paper was mounted in the foyer and was titled,
'Found January 2, 2021'

It was certainly his note, his handwriting and fingerprints were checked, too! It began casually: *Before I write this for anyone who might come across it (having already bound 52 pages.) Hope this is found by the time of our eminent rescue.*

Hello To Anyone Reading This:

Happy Data Collecting!

Cultural observation will survive within any democratic society valuing science. And truth. Record keeping is important! Always be learning, much phenomenon is not understood – It's simply among us. Accept the process of discovery.

Together we'll comprehend more and welcome opportunities to scrutinize, inside and out, to your heart's content.

Continue cherishing learning progression. Become part of a reviewed process; examine it, wear it. Perfect answers are rarely readily available. All won't always agree.

I believe a veil exists between life and what we

188

call death. I cannot doubt it. Reputable research data reports in our country, most believe in spirits and an afterlife.

Honor ourselves in this life. Reexamine our fingerprinted views while we're living. Commit to the truth of and within in our soul.

All must be allowed this. I will close but first share that recently I heard vocals say "calm" and the word "acceptance" and both were uttered in three other languages (that I only barely understood), i.e. 'Annahme,' and 'Yanshou'. (I still am unable to look up translations and meanings). Later, the words 'beauty is inside' and 'richness is inside' but they too were very faint. Also, "The Way" was heard by all of us.

After I awoke from my dream last night, all five, were singing in English: "We come unseen from everywhere to help and to comfort you."

Move forward. Acknowledge what obstructs your peace, feel it deeply to understand it, but make it leave. Love is for you to know inside yourself. Loving yourself is important for moving forward. Respect Others and Respect Yourself. Know there's love.

Time and Space are one and will not end. Move within. More With Truth,

Dr. Michael Merrick, Professor, PhD

Until we meet again,
BE Love,

Dr. Professor Wrecked Van Camper,
Michael Merrick

Time and Space. Can They Exist Without the Other? What's the Difference?

Space and time are two fundamental concepts that shape our understanding of the universe. While **space** refers to the three-dimensional extent in which objects and events exist, **time** represents the progression of events from the past through the present to the future. Both **space** and **time** are interconnected, ***forming the fabric of spacetime***, as described by Einstein's theory of general relativity.

They are inseparable and influence each other, with the curvature of spacetime affecting the motion of objects within it. While space provides the stage for events to unfold, time allows us to perceive and measure the duration and sequence of these events. Together, space and time form the foundation of our perception and exploration of the cosmos.

By Franz Kapfa

"I am constantly trying to communicate

something incommunicable, to explain something inexplainable, [and to tell] something I only feel in my bones - which can only be experienced in those bones.

Spirit melodies are not material sound waves, but spirit pulsations received by the spirits of celestial personalities. There is a vastness of range and a soul of expression, as well as a grandeur of execution, associated with the melody of the spheres, which are wholly beyond human comprehension. I have seen millions of enraptured beings held in sublime ecstasy while the melody of the realm rolled in upon the spirit energy of the celestial circuits. These marvelous melodies can be broadcast to the uttermost realms of the universe.

Partial excerpt: URANTIA Paper 44

Please see, in the next few pages, a little guide for each subject. First, terms and examples in reasoning and logic. Seven steps of scientific study building. A bit of chemistry,

Logic vs. Reason
What's the Difference?

*Logic and reason are closely related concepts, but they have distinct differences. **LOGIC** refers to the systematic and structured approach to thinking and reasoning, often involving the use of formal rules and principles. It focuses on the validity and coherence of arguments, aiming to find and eliminate fallacies or inconsistencies.*

*On the other hand, **REASON** is a broader term encompassing the ability to think, understand, and make judgments based on logical thinking. rationality, evidence, and critical thinking. While logic provides a* framework for reasoning, reason is the cognitive process that uses logic to reach sound and justified conclusions.

Key Logical Terms – Beginners

Premise *Serves as a basis for an argument or an inference. Used to support a conclusion in an argument.*

Proposition*: A declarative statement that is either true or false, but not both. It is the broad category that includes all statements, including premises.*

Role In **Arguments** *Premises are the statements that provide the evidence or reasons to establish the truth or a conclusion. Proposannitions can stand alone as statements that express a truth value.*

    Conclusion*: judgement or decision reached by reasoning. Validity: property of an argument where if the premises are true, the conclusion must also be true.*

https//: Thisvsthat.io

An inference is a conclusion *drawn from evidenc e ,,,,…or reasoning. Here are some examples:*

Cause-and-effect reasoning *looks for relationships where one event causes another.*

Inductive reasoning *draws conclusions from specific observations*

  Understanding logical clauses *is essential for fields like computer science and mathematics.*

Conditional Statements*: "If-then" statements that express a relationship between propositions.*

 Quantifiers*: Terms like "all," "some," or "none" that specify the quantity of subjects in a statement.*

Conjecture *is when an opinion or conclusion is formed based on incomplete information.*

SEVEN Study Building
Steps of the Scientific Method

Conducting a scientific study and are as follows:

Ask a Question: *Identify a problem or inquiry. sparking curiosity.*

Do Background Research: *Gather info what is already known about your question.*

Formulate a Hypothesis:

> *Based on research and your understanding of the total situation, first take an educated guess what might happen during a studied experiment*

Design and Conduct an Experiment:

> *Create an experiment, then test your hypothesis while controlling variables e ffectively.*

Collect and Analyze Data: *Record observations & measurements during your experiment systematically.*

Draw Conclusions: *Evaluate whether your data supports or refutes your hypothesis.*

Communication Results. *Share findings through reports, presentations, or publications so others can review and replicate the work.*

These above steps "ensure" that conclusions are based on empirical evidence rather than speculation, and they play a critical role in transforming curiosity into verifiable knowledge.

MATTER and SPIRIT

Matter and spirit are two fundamental aspects of existence often seen as opposing forces. Matter refers to the physical substance making up all the world around us, while spirit is tied to an image of the intangible essence of a person or being.

While matter is tangible, and can be physically touched, as tactile, it can be measured and seen, while spirit is often imagined as elusive and difficult to define.

Both matter and spirit happen to be, --- according to most philosophers and scientists --- interconnected.

They shape our understanding of the world and our place within it.

If there is thought to be a relationship between matter and spirit (as theologians might pronounce). Their dual existence around us is complex and multifaceted, each influencing and shaping the other in profound ways.

(thisvsthat.io)

195

CHEMISTRY

My Dear Learners. If you don't have a clue about elements and atoms and molecules, here is a little something to start with. And I say that in the grand scheme of matter, it's very little. With eternal Love to you in all this timespace. Amen. Anthony

A Brief Chemistry Lesson from Anthony

Atoms and molecules are both fundamental units of matter but differ in composition and structure. An atom is the smallest indivisible unit of an element, consisting of a nucleus having protons and neutrons, surrounded by electrons. At ENERGY LEVELS. On the other hand, a molecule is a group of two or more atoms held together by chemical bonds.

While atoms can exist independently, it's molecules that require the presence of multiple atoms to form. Additionally, atoms are identified by their atomic number, which determines their element, while molecules are identified by their chemical formula, representing the types and number of atoms present.

Overall, atoms are the building blocks of molecules, understanding their properties and interactions is crucial in understanding the behavior of matter.

Atom and element are both fundamental concepts in chemistry. An atom is the smallest unit of matter that keeps the properties of an element. An atom consists of a nucleus having protons and neutrons, surrounded by electrons. An element, on the other hand, is a pure substance made up of only one type of atom.

.Wikipedia and https://thisvsthat.io

The importance is carbon has 6 = 2 in 1s and 4 MORE which creates bonds with so many things it is the basis for all life as we know it.

It was alluded to in the story that there might have been an unablated element which found its way to earth. There are nuclear reactions in the celestial heavenly layers – through an area so vast *it stays beyond our imaginations.*

Also, it has been discussed, what is fission? Fission and fusion are two different processes that release energy, but they occur in opposite ways. Fission involves the splitting of a heavy atomic nucleus into two smaller nuclei, releasing a large amount of energy in the process. This process is used in nuclear power plants and atomic bombs. On the other hand, fusion involves the combining of two light atomic nuclei to form a heavier nucleus, also releasing a tremendous amount of energy. Again, note, that another atom acts as a helper temporarily to facilitate that fusion reaction.

. To understand how elements from other galaxies could land on Earth, consider: metallic particles float in the atmosphere, sometime land on earth? To understand the presence of metallic particles floating in space, consider the following points:

- ***Fission and Fusion Defined****: Fission splits heavy atomic nuclei, while fusion combines light nuclei to form heavier ones.*

- ***Cosmic Origins****: Metallic particles in space primarily originate from supernova explosions and stellar processes, not fission or fusion.*

- ***Stellar Nucleosynthesis****: Fusion in stars creates heavier elements, which can be released into space when stars die.*

- ***Supernova Contributions****: Fission is not a significant process in space, instead, supernovae disperse metallic elements formed through fusion.*

- ***Interstellar Medium****: Metallic particles are part of the interstellar medium, resulting from stellar evolution and not from fission reactions.*

- ***Astrophysical Processes****: The formation of metallic particles is linked to astrophysical processes rather than nuclear fission or fusion directly.*

- ***Solar Wind:*** *Charged particles from the sun can carry elements from other celestial bodies and deposit them on Earth.*

197

- **Cosmic Dust:** Tiny particles from space can enter Earth's atmosphere …Meteorites: Fragments of asteroids or comets can break off and travel.
- **Space Missions:** Human-made spacecraft can collect samples

If we get that far.

Metely explained with love again, Professor Anthony

==

LUMINSTRATUM

David Anthony: Take metallurgy, again. The branch concerned with properties of metals, those many rare earth metals? Well, My Lady, if you were to associate chemistry to my life while I knew Mary, I would be known as a meson.

My Lady: Do you mean a meson, like the reactionary sub atomic intermediate mass between, say, an electron and a proton which transmits the strong interaction that binds nucleons together in the atomic nucleus?

David Anthony: Wow, My Lady, I am impressed! When did you have time to absorb that bit of info in your spiritual gift box? No, won't make it on a periodic table because it is hadronic subatomic particle, not an element.

My Lady: Yes, not an unnamed bit of metallic element still needing a place. Some addendum periodic table. And it is amazing what and who you are, what you were. Dave, the teacher! You are the father of --

David Anthony: Ah, yes, you know me now! You did before, too! We have our story there, My Lady, to share if wanted.

My Lady: Has Mary recognized you now during these last few months?

David Anthony: That's for her to share and me to know.

You know, the instrument sounds that Dr. Merrick heard……. not naming …. It is past time for all interested in the WVC to accept that they are part of spirit melodies that somehow became capsulized in the cave during the fated time, ready to join the clamor of the trees beaten down

Creative thinker for a mere celestial, you think?

My Lady: Oh, I question if you can ever adequately solve this. Spirit business is summoning you now to be with the ladies at the Illumined Home who, for hours after you stop your sweet whisper, will continue smiling in their sleep.

David Anthony: You mean feel the Good Vibrations?

My Lady: Well, what matter could you ever add?

David Anthony: That's a loaded question. I have no matter.

But guess what, My Lady. As you do, I do have love and truth.

Love vs. Truth
What's the Difference?

Love and truth are both major realities to be aware of during human existence! Often, they exist in tension with one another.

Love - emotions, compassion, and connection

Truth - Linked to facts, honesty, and objectivity.

While love can sometimes cloud our judgment and lead us to overlook some truths we'd prefer not to see, and truth can at times – often, actually - be harsh and difficult to accept. Both love and truth provide us with a sense of purpose, finding a balance is essential to happiness.

*AB*OUT THE AUTHOR

Makenlief.com is the author's website.
Darla is a member of the Warner Springs Artisan Guild, is a graduate from SDSU, Communications, Journalism and P.R. While employed at a community college reading services department she worked weekends volunteering in trauma support. After losing her husband, she became a Certified Grief Educator and helps the newly grieved by working art with conversation on zoom. Facebook can be found on darla@makenlief.

Another Elementary Luminary branch off this novella will be published, showcasing and connecting a story on many Squib Books from the Illumined Home in Illumined Town – the story's staff, volunteers, student interviewers, and writers give seniors a platformed voice, with their guardians (and Sentinels) who thoroughly own their own truth.